HER LAST

CHOICE

(A Rachel Gift Mystery—Book Five)

BLAKE PIERCE

Blake Pierce

Blake Pierce is the USA Today bestselling author of the RILEY PAGE mystery series, which includes seventeen books. Blake Pierce is also the author of the MACKENZIE WHITE mystery series, comprising fourteen books; of the AVERY BLACK mystery series, comprising six books; of the KERI LOCKE mystery series, comprising five books; of the MAKING OF RILEY PAIGE mystery series, comprising six books; of the KATE WISE mystery series, comprising seven books; of the CHLOE FINE psychological suspense mystery, comprising six books; of the JESSE HUNT psychological suspense thriller series, comprising twenty four books; of the AU PAIR psychological suspense thriller series, comprising three books; of the ZOE PRIME mystery series, comprising six books; of the ADELE SHARP mystery series, comprising fifteen books, of the EUROPEAN VOYAGE cozy mystery series, comprising four books; of the new LAURA FROST FBI suspense thriller, comprising nine books (and counting); of the new ELLA DARK FBI suspense thriller, comprising eleven books (and counting); of the A YEAR IN EUROPE cozy mystery series, comprising nine books, of the AVA GOLD mystery series, comprising six books (and counting); of the RACHEL GIFT mystery series, comprising eight books (and counting); of the VALERIE LAW mystery series, comprising nine books (and counting); of the PAIGE KING mystery series, comprising six books (and counting); of the MAY MOORE mystery series, comprising six books (and counting); and the CORA SHIELDS mystery series, comprising three books (and counting).

An avid reader and lifelong fan of the mystery and thriller genres, Blake loves to hear from you, so please feel free to visit www.blakepierceauthor.com to learn more and stay in touch.

ISBN: 978-1-0943-7751-3

BOOKS BY BLAKE PIERCE

CORA SHIELDS MYSTERY SERIES
UNDONE (Book #1)
UNWANTED (Book #2)
UNHINGED (Book #3)

MAY MOORE SUSPENSE THRILLER
NEVER RUN (Book #1)
NEVER TELL (Book #2)
NEVER LIVE (Book #3)
NEVER HIDE (Book #4)
NEVER FORGIVE (Book #5)
NEVER AGAIN (Book #6)

PAIGE KING MYSTERY SERIES
THE GIRL HE PINED (Book #1)
THE GIRL HE CHOSE (Book #2)
THE GIRL HE TOOK (Book #3)
THE GIRL HE WISHED (Book #4)
THE GIRL HE CROWNED (Book #5)
THE GIRL HE WATCHED (Book #6)

VALERIE LAW MYSTERY SERIES
NO MERCY (Book #1)
NO PITY (Book #2)
NO FEAR (Book #3)
NO SLEEP (Book #4)
NO QUARTER (Book #5)
NO CHANCE (Book #6)
NO REFUGE (Book #7)
NO GRACE (Book #8)
NO ESCAPE (Book #9)

RACHEL GIFT MYSTERY SERIES
HER LAST WISH (Book #1)
HER LAST CHANCE (Book #2)
HER LAST HOPE (Book #3)
HER LAST FEAR (Book #4)

HER LAST CHOICE (Book #5)
HER LAST BREATH (Book #6)
HER LAST MISTAKE (Book #7)
HER LAST DESIRE (Book #8)

AVA GOLD MYSTERY SERIES
CITY OF PREY (Book #1)
CITY OF FEAR (Book #2)
CITY OF BONES (Book #3)
CITY OF GHOSTS (Book #4)
CITY OF DEATH (Book #5)
CITY OF VICE (Book #6)

A YEAR IN EUROPE
A MURDER IN PARIS (Book #1)
DEATH IN FLORENCE (Book #2)
VENGEANCE IN VIENNA (Book #3)
A FATALITY IN SPAIN (Book #4)

ELLA DARK FBI SUSPENSE THRILLER
GIRL, ALONE (Book #1)
GIRL, TAKEN (Book #2)
GIRL, HUNTED (Book #3)
GIRL, SILENCED (Book #4)
GIRL, VANISHED (Book 5)
GIRL ERASED (Book #6)
GIRL, FORSAKEN (Book #7)
GIRL, TRAPPED (Book #8)
GIRL, EXPENDABLE (Book #9)
GIRL, ESCAPED (Book #10)
GIRL, HIS (Book #11)

LAURA FROST FBI SUSPENSE THRILLER
ALREADY GONE (Book #1)
ALREADY SEEN (Book #2)
ALREADY TRAPPED (Book #3)
ALREADY MISSING (Book #4)
ALREADY DEAD (Book #5)
ALREADY TAKEN (Book #6)
ALREADY CHOSEN (Book #7)
ALREADY LOST (Book #8)

ALREADY HIS (Book #9)

EUROPEAN VOYAGE COZY MYSTERY SERIES
MURDER (AND BAKLAVA) (Book #1)
DEATH (AND APPLE STRUDEL) (Book #2)
CRIME (AND LAGER) (Book #3)
MISFORTUNE (AND GOUDA) (Book #4)
CALAMITY (AND A DANISH) (Book #5)
MAYHEM (AND HERRING) (Book #6)

ADELE SHARP MYSTERY SERIES
LEFT TO DIE (Book #1)
LEFT TO RUN (Book #2)
LEFT TO HIDE (Book #3)
LEFT TO KILL (Book #4)
LEFT TO MURDER (Book #5)
LEFT TO ENVY (Book #6)
LEFT TO LAPSE (Book #7)
LEFT TO VANISH (Book #8)
LEFT TO HUNT (Book #9)
LEFT TO FEAR (Book #10)
LEFT TO PREY (Book #11)
LEFT TO LURE (Book #12)
LEFT TO CRAVE (Book #13)
LEFT TO LOATHE (Book #14)
LEFT TO HARM (Book #15)

THE AU PAIR SERIES
ALMOST GONE (Book#1)
ALMOST LOST (Book #2)
ALMOST DEAD (Book #3)

ZOE PRIME MYSTERY SERIES
FACE OF DEATH (Book#1)
FACE OF MURDER (Book #2)
FACE OF FEAR (Book #3)
FACE OF MADNESS (Book #4)
FACE OF FURY (Book #5)
FACE OF DARKNESS (Book #6)

A JESSIE HUNT PSYCHOLOGICAL SUSPENSE SERIES

THE PERFECT WIFE (Book #1)
THE PERFECT BLOCK (Book #2)
THE PERFECT HOUSE (Book #3)
THE PERFECT SMILE (Book #4)
THE PERFECT LIE (Book #5)
THE PERFECT LOOK (Book #6)
THE PERFECT AFFAIR (Book #7)
THE PERFECT ALIBI (Book #8)
THE PERFECT NEIGHBOR (Book #9)
THE PERFECT DISGUISE (Book #10)
THE PERFECT SECRET (Book #11)
THE PERFECT FAÇADE (Book #12)
THE PERFECT IMPRESSION (Book #13)
THE PERFECT DECEIT (Book #14)
THE PERFECT MISTRESS (Book #15)
THE PERFECT IMAGE (Book #16)
THE PERFECT VEIL (Book #17)
THE PERFECT INDISCRETION (Book #18)
THE PERFECT RUMOR (Book #19)
THE PERFECT COUPLE (Book #20)
THE PERFECT MURDER (Book #21)
THE PERFECT HUSBAND (Book #22)
THE PERFECT SCANDAL (Book #23)
THE PERFECT MASK (Book #24)

CHLOE FINE PSYCHOLOGICAL SUSPENSE SERIES
NEXT DOOR (Book #1)
A NEIGHBOR'S LIE (Book #2)
CUL DE SAC (Book #3)
SILENT NEIGHBOR (Book #4)
HOMECOMING (Book #5)
TINTED WINDOWS (Book #6)

KATE WISE MYSTERY SERIES
IF SHE KNEW (Book #1)
IF SHE SAW (Book #2)
IF SHE RAN (Book #3)
IF SHE HID (Book #4)
IF SHE FLED (Book #5)
IF SHE FEARED (Book #6)

IF SHE HEARD (Book #7)

THE MAKING OF RILEY PAIGE SERIES
WATCHING (Book #1)
WAITING (Book #2)
LURING (Book #3)
TAKING (Book #4)
STALKING (Book #5)
KILLING (Book #6)

RILEY PAIGE MYSTERY SERIES
ONCE GONE (Book #1)
ONCE TAKEN (Book #2)
ONCE CRAVED (Book #3)
ONCE LURED (Book #4)
ONCE HUNTED (Book #5)
ONCE PINED (Book #6)
ONCE FORSAKEN (Book #7)
ONCE COLD (Book #8)
ONCE STALKED (Book #9)
ONCE LOST (Book #10)
ONCE BURIED (Book #11)
ONCE BOUND (Book #12)
ONCE TRAPPED (Book #13)
ONCE DORMANT (Book #14)
ONCE SHUNNED (Book #15)
ONCE MISSED (Book #16)
ONCE CHOSEN (Book #17)

MACKENZIE WHITE MYSTERY SERIES
BEFORE HE KILLS (Book #1)
BEFORE HE SEES (Book #2)
BEFORE HE COVETS (Book #3)
BEFORE HE TAKES (Book #4)
BEFORE HE NEEDS (Book #5)
BEFORE HE FEELS (Book #6)
BEFORE HE SINS (Book #7)
BEFORE HE HUNTS (Book #8)
BEFORE HE PREYS (Book #9)
BEFORE HE LONGS (Book #10)
BEFORE HE LAPSES (Book #11)

BEFORE HE ENVIES (Book #12)
BEFORE HE STALKS (Book #13)
BEFORE HE HARMS (Book #14)

AVERY BLACK MYSTERY SERIES
CAUSE TO KILL (Book #1)
CAUSE TO RUN (Book #2)
CAUSE TO HIDE (Book #3)
CAUSE TO FEAR (Book #4)
CAUSE TO SAVE (Book #5)
CAUSE TO DREAD (Book #6)

KERI LOCKE MYSTERY SERIES
A TRACE OF DEATH (Book #1)
A TRACE OF MURDER (Book #2)
A TRACE OF VICE (Book #3)
A TRACE OF CRIME (Book #4)
A TRACE OF HOPE (Book #5)

CHAPTER ONE

The universe wasn't a rational or fair place. Polly Warren knew this better than anyone. If the universe had any sense of cosmic justice, she wouldn't have breast cancer. If the world was just, she'd have a caregiver who lived closer than two hours away. If the world was just, she wouldn't be a twenty-six-year-old with breast cancer, single, alone, and, as of two weeks ago, without a job.

It was nearing five o'clock, and Polly Warren knew that she was going to get stuck in afternoon traffic. She just knew it. It wasn't the best way to end an already awful day but she supposed it could be worse. After all, she'd just finished her third cycle of chemotherapy. In a just universe, she'd be able to skip all the traffic, return home, enjoy a glass of wine, and conk out in front of a trashy reality show.

The one caregiver she did have was her sister, who lived in the town of Poquoson—almost two hours outside of Richmond, a bit shy of Norfolk. She'd come with Polly to the first several treatments, but when it had become clear that Polly's side effects were minimal, Polly had insisted she stop making the drive every time she had an appointment. After each treatment, Polly spent forty-five minutes watching YouTube clips on her phone to make sure she was okay to drive home. And not a single time had she had any sort of serious side effects.

She had a brother, too, and he lived locally—just a fifteen-minute drive up the road. But he'd seen this cancer kill their mother and he'd kept his distance from Polly ever since her diagnosis. No big deal, really, as Kevin had distanced himself from the family for about a decade or so now. She hadn't even seen him in over three years.

Secretly, though, she was glad. Kevin being around as she was going through this would make it even harder and much more stressful. As for her sister, she'd asked her not to come anymore because there was something about her presence and help that made Polly feel uncharacteristically weak. It was bad enough that she had to deal with the fact that she had cancer, but having someone there to walk her through it and hold her hand was sort of demeaning in a way she couldn't quite grasp. And Polly knew that if she was going to beat this, she was going to have to keep a positive mindset about the whole thing.

Though the doctors were not giving any sort of news or updates to make her think she *would* beat it. In fact, Polly knew her chances of surviving were slim.

Polly walked to her car, on the western edge of the hospital parking lot. Even from there, not yet in her car and looking out to the highway, she could see the looming lines of rush hour traffic. She started to wonder if maybe she'd stop by that little Japanese hibachi place just down the road and wait out the traffic there with some sushi.

It was another example of trying to keep a positive mindset, of not letting a cancer diagnosis tear her down.

She had nearly approached her car when she heard her name. It was from a sweet-sounding voice, coming from somewhere nearby.

"Polly?"

She paused and looked to the right. There was a man about her age walking toward her. He looked shy and quite handsome. He had shaggy brown hair, a five o'clock shadow, and a crooked smile. It was the smile that stopped her. It was the sort of smile that would have won her over without a word back in the days when she used to frequent bars and clubs.

"Hi…?" she said. "Do I know you?"

The grin got wider. She thought she should know him. If she'd ever met a guy that looked like this, with a smile like that, she was pretty sure she'd remember him.

"Well, I'd hope you would," he said. "It's going to hurt my feelings a bit if you don't remember me."

She cocked her head and returned his smile. She felt a bit weak because of the treatment but apparently, it did nothing to curb her interest in cute men. "Maybe," she said. "I'm sorry, I'm just a little out of sorts from an appointment I just had. We've met before?"

He chuckled and looked to the ground. "We have. And apparently, it wasn't very memorable."

"Well, what's your na—"

The punch came out of nowhere. By the time Polly attempted to take a step back, she realized it wasn't going to be just a punch. No, the handsome man's hand came up and over in an arc, as if he were about to chop firewood. And just before he landed the blow, Polly saw something small and shiny in his hand. The handle to something? A bar, a lead pipe…?

She didn't know. What she did know was when the object struck her head, the world went black. She fell to the ground, her head a wall of pain. She knew when the second blow came, but she didn't feel it; she simply heard it, a soft and crunching sort of sound.

Maybe there would be a third one, too. But if it came, she was not aware.

She was dead half a breath after the second.

CHAPTER TWO

Rachel sat in the same chair she always sat in when she visited Director Anderson's office. She'd lost count of how many times she'd used it over the course of her decade or so with the bureau. She'd had some tense meetings and brutal debriefs in this chair, but she'd never felt the insane amount of tension in the room as she did right now.

She knew what she was about to demand, and she would not waver from it. She was, in a very real way, about to play a high-stakes game of poker with him. She knew that Anderson already knew some of her cards but he didn't know she was sick—that there was an inoperable tumor slowly invading her brain. That was her ace-in-the-hole. And if she played her hand right, she may just get what she wanted today without having to tell him.

"I appreciate you meeting with me, sir," Rachel said.

"Of course. I know…well, I can understand how the past few days have been hard on you."

"That's good to hear. Because you know me, sir. I don't waste time beating around the bush. And I suspect you already know why I'm here."

Director Anderson nodded and steepled his fingers together on his desk. "Yes, I suppose I do. And quite frankly, I'm surprised it took you this long to come to me. All the same…I'd like for you to formally make the request."

She wasted no time. Hell, she'd already wasted two days. "I want to be the one the bureau sends after Lynch. I know you haven't already tasked an agent with it, and I want it."

"Agent Gift, you know I can't allow that."

"No, I don't. I know you think it's a bad idea, but you can allow it."

The subject rested between them like an invisible bomb—a bomb with the name of Alex Lynch. The man she'd put away years ago who had sharpened a grudge against her. A man who had somehow managed to taunt her and her family from within prison walls, including paying someone to deliver a dead squirrel and a threatening note into her daughter's bedroom. And now a man who possessed the determination and tenacity to somehow escape from prison was moving around the state, free and on the roam.

"Well, here's the thing," Anderson said. "You're right. I do think it's a bad idea to let you anywhere near it. Your personal involvement with Alex Lynch makes you a very bad candidate for the job. And don't you go thinking for a minute that I haven't yet assigned anyone because I was waiting for you. It's quite the opposite, in fact. The US Marshals Service is already involved on this. They're on the hunt."

"I figured they would be," Rachel said. "Two days in and what results do they have?"

"They have a few leads, as a matter of fact. From what I was told this morning, they are following a trail that is leading them to Charlottesville. Lynch has a sick mother there, you know."

"I do. And if you think a monster like Alex Lynch gives a damn about his ailing mother, you're as sorely misled as the US Marshals Service. I know Lynch. I know him *too* well."

"You know I can't put you on this, Rachel."

Using her first name…that said a lot. He felt for her. It showed her that Anderson wanted her on it, but knew it was a dead end. "Even if I ignored all instincts and signed you on to it, you know what would happen, right? As soon as the US Marshals run into you, they'll block you at every turn."

"Then I just won't run into them."

Anderson shook his head. "My answer is no. You're too emotionally involved. The way he's messed with your family over these last few weeks…I just can't allow it."

Rachel saw the dead squirrel in her daughter's room, placed there by one of Lynch's old friends. She recalled how upset her Grandma Tate had been when she'd gotten the letter from Lynch in the mail, informing her of Rachel's diagnosis. Yes, she *was* emotionally attached to the case. Yes, she was taking it personally.

"So there's nothing I can say to make you put me on this?" she asked.

"No," he said. "I'm sorry, Rachel. But I can't."

She sighed, nodded, and got to her feet. "Then I'd like to put in for a leave of absence, effective immediately."

The look on his face was not one of shock, as she'd expected, but befuddlement. If it *were* a game of poker, she'd just made a wager that he'd not been expecting. What he didn't know, though, was that he could not make any sort of countermove. No upping the bet, no calling her bluff. Because she'd already made the decision.

Going after Alex Lynch would have been her last case. After that, she'd give her notice and live the last few healthy months she had with her family.

And if she wasn't going to get Lynch, then she was done.

"Rachel…Agent Gift, what are you trying to do?"

"I'm not trying to do anything," Rachel said. "But with Lynch out, there's no way I'm going to be able to focus on anything else. So I'm going to spend time with my family until he's caught. In the past five weeks, Lynch has had an effect on my daughter, my grandmother, and the overall safety of my family. So if I can't go after Lynch, I'm taking the time to be with my family."

Rachel studied Anderson's face, trying to decide how he was feeling about this. There was scrutiny at first, as if he thought he might be getting played or manipulated. After a few seconds, he got to his feet and looked her directly in the eyes.

"What else is going on here, Gift?"

"Nothing. I just think this is the best move for my family right now." And on the end of that, she felt the weight of what she had left to tell him. She could tell him about her tumor and it would all make sense to him. But for now, she wanted to keep that away from him and, truth be told, she wasn't quite sure why. Maybe it was because she'd feel like she was exploiting her weakness and now, sitting here with him, that seemed like a very cowardly thing to do. But really, at the core of it, she knew the simple truth: she didn't want to appear weak in any way. Especially not to Director Anderson.

"How long of a leave of absence are you talking about?"

"I don't know. How long do you think it will take the US Marshals to do their job?"

Anderson folded his arms across his chest. It was a posture that reminded her how, even though he was nearing sixty, the man was in excellent shape. His arms and chest filled out the white button-down nicely.

"I'll give you two weeks," he said. "Anything more than that, we need to touch base."

"I certainly hope it won't take them that long." Immature or not, she just couldn't resist getting in that last jab.

"Agent Gift, are you sure about this?"

She glared at him for a moment. It was clear he knew he didn't have the entire story but, given the tricky nature of the situation, was choosing to remain quiet about it.

"Yes," Rachel said. "I'm positive. Only…would you mind letting me know when they find him? Can I stay updated?"

Anderson considered it for a moment and finally nodded. "I'll send you any daily reports pertaining to the pursuit of Alex Lynch, yes."

"Thank you."

She made her way to the door and was surprised to find that she felt a slight bit of regret. She felt that she was indeed manipulating Anderson in a way, pressing him into a *give me what I want or I may just walk* sort of scenario. But then again, he didn't know about the tumor, about the fact that she likely only had a year to live—and half of that time may be spent in considerable stress and pain.

But she said nothing else as she left his office. She figured he'd have someone email her the paperwork necessary for her two weeks of leave, but that could be handled later. For now, she had a date with her daughter and grandmother to get to.

She couldn't think of a better way to start her two weeks off. And after all, maybe it would distract her from the unsettling fact that as of right now, she was on leave from the FBI.

CHAPTER THREE

It was an overcast day, a breeze passing through the park as if reminding everyone that autumn was on its way. Rachel walked along one of the many sidewalks that led through the park, with her daughter to her left and her grandmother on the other side of Paige. They'd just left the ice cream truck, all three of them carrying their own treats. Paige had a bit of her cotton-candy-flavored soft serve trickling down her arm.

"Okay," Rachel said, looking at Paige. "You took the day off from school, you went to the pool with Grandma Tate, you got ice cream, and we're having pizza for dinner. Is there anything else you want to do?"

Paige thought about it for a moment as she licked her ice cream cone. With wide eyes she said, "Is this the park Daddy sometimes took me to? The one with the duck pond?"

"It is."

"Ooh, can we go see the ducks?"

"I don't see why not."

Grandma Tate seemed to be just as overjoyed as Paige at this news. She clapped her hands excitedly, almost dropping her ice cream. "I wonder if they have anything to feed them!"

"Let's go see," Rachel said.

As they rerouted themselves and went off in search of the duck pond, Rachel couldn't help but feel a bit guilty. It was a gorgeous afternoon and a very touching moment for the three of them, but her mind was partially back on her meeting with Anderson. She couldn't help but wonder if there might be some repercussions waiting for her if she chose to go back.

Only, you're not going back, she thought to herself. *Whether or not Lynch is caught, you can't go back. If you do, you'll have to reveal your diagnosis eventually. You were already a ticking time bomb on the last few cases since you got the diagnosis.*

This was easier to admit to herself now that Jack, her partner, knew. He'd been understanding and even helpful, referring her to a doctor who had managed to give her a bit of hope for a small amount of time. Jack knew, Grandma Tate knew, and now Paige knew. Peter, her husband, knew as well. But they'd been separated for about a month now, and living without him in the wake of all of this had been far easier than she'd expected.

She was still at odds with the fact that Paige knew. She'd taken it as well as could be expected for a girl of eight years of age to take such news. There had been some crying, sure, but there had mostly been a relentless barrage of questions. Most of the time, though, things with Paige had been mostly normal ever since Rachel had told her. Like now, as the duck pond came into view and the little girl pulled both her mother and her grandmother toward the water. The ducks, having long since grown accustomed to the presence of humans, scattered listlessly, some retreating and some swimming forward in the hope of snacks.

"Look at that," Grandma Tate said. She was pointing to a small dispenser by the edge of a little dock that extended out over the pond. It contained little pellets for the ducks. She dug into her purse, grabbed two quarters, and sent Paige out to the dock to get some.

Rachel sat on one of the several benches around the pond, watching her daughter hurry along up to the dock. Grandma Tate sat as well, giving Rachel a reassuring slap on the knee.

"You doing okay?"

"Yes, I'm fine."

"You're sure? I'm certain that meeting with your director couldn't have been easy on you."

"It was actually easier than I'd thought it would be."

She'd gotten used to this over the past two weeks. Now that Grandma Tate knew about the tumor, she'd been doting over her incessantly. *Do you need anything? Shouldn't you be resting? Are you feeling well?* On and on and on.

Rachel supposed part of it came from a strange dichotomy between them, wherein Grandma Tate had been diagnosed before Rachel but the treatments she was taking were helping and her cancer was going into remission. In a relationship where Rachel, the granddaughter, was fully intending to have to take care of Grandma Tate, the roles had been quickly reversed. Both women were very much aware of this odd reversal of fortune, and it resulted in a strange little dance.

On the dock, Paige had gotten the pellets for the ducks. She'd placed them into a plastic container by the dispenser and was shaking it joyously at her mother and great-grandmother.

"Well, we'd better get over there before she shakes the whole dock down," Grandma Tate said. She got up and started in that direction but turned back to Rachel. "You're okay with the rest of your days being like this?"

Rachel saw the glimmer of tears in her grandmother's eyes. But she also saw her daughter, bright and beaming by the pond with sticky ice cream trails on her forearms. She saw the afternoon light coming down across the trees and over the pond. It all seemed to make the idea of Alex Lynch seem abstract. It made her career as an FBI agent seem like a very vivid dream she'd once had, even so soon removed from Anderson's office.

"Yeah, I think so," she said.

Grandma Tate nodded and looked back over to Paige. "You coming?" she asked Rachel.

"Yeah. Just…give me a second."

Grandma Tate walked over to the dock and joined Paige. Rachel watched them for a moment, generational bookends that helped her to get a better grasp on the flow and depth of life. She'd opted not to go out and join them just yet because she wasn't quite sure she'd answered her grandmother's question as honestly as she should have.

Because the truth of the matter was that she wasn't sure if she could spend the rest of her days like this. Even if she got motivated and pulled out her very short bucket list, traveling while she still could, she wasn't sure she'd be satisfied. While she'd meant everything she told Director Anderson earlier in the day, the idea of just coasting through during her last few healthy months felt like defeat. The competitive and determined part of her wanted to run until the wheels came off, to keep working until she couldn't get out of bed in the morning.

And if Anderson had caved and placed her on the Alex Lynch case, she supposed that's exactly what she would have done.

Defeat or not, the sting of it lessened when she looked at Paige, though. A girl who was going to have to grow up without a mother—and with a father who was probably going to be processing guilt and a series of what-ifs for most of his daughter's childhood.

So maybe these last few days shouldn't be all about her. Maybe she should focus them around Paige. Maybe she should let Paige know how much she was loved and that even in the face of an approaching death, there was nothing that could separate Paige from the love her mother felt for her.

Looking out, she watched Paige and Grandma Tate start tossing out pellets to the ducks. Paige giggled and laughed as the ducks came rocketing over, skimming effortlessly over the water. Slowly, Rachel stood and made her way over. As she did, her heart beamed with love for the two people standing in front of her, even as she could also feel the slight shadow of a raincloud over her every thought, a cloud that cast a shadow of doubt—a shadow that she imagined likely took the shape of Alex Lynch.

CHAPTER FOUR

Jack Rivers sat at his cubicle, looking at the phone number he'd scrawled down earlier in the day. It was just a series of numbers, but looking at them made him feel nervous. He'd found this particular phone number after a week or so of searching and now that he had it, he wasn't sure what he should do with it. He'd written it down because he'd not felt safe keeping the digital record of it. He'd had to go outside of the bureau for help in tracking the number down and, as such, did not want to get into any sort of trouble—not just for the secondary, under-the-table help, but also because he'd been using bureau time and resources on information-gathering that had not been related to a case.

Well, he'd crossed the line now, he supposed. Might as well take it a step further. Besides, he knew Anderson had no idea and anyone higher up than Anderson typically didn't involve themselves in the day-to-day actions of a lowly agent like Jack Rivers.

He picked up his cellphone—his personal one, not the bureau-assigned one—and his finger hovered over the face of it for a moment before he punched the number in. The bit of remaining hesitancy didn't come from his worries about being reprimanded, but of how Rachel might respond. He was doing this for her, and she had no idea what he was up to. She might find it an invasion of her personal space, or simply a part of her life he had no business delving into.

But again…he had the number. He'd made some shady moves to get it. Why back out now?

Still, not here…not at his cubicle where anyone could walk by and hear the conversation he was about to have. He hopped up out of his chair and made his way out of the central area of the field office. He walked down the hall, out of the front lobby, and to the small lawn outside. Only one other person was out here, an agent by the name of Carter, sneaking in a quick cigarette. The two men nodded to one another as Jack walked past him and to a bench that looked right back toward the FBI's Richmond field office.

Before he could convince himself to stall again, Jack punched the number into his phone. It rang once, twice, and was picked up on the third ring.

"Hello?" said a gruff, male voice.

"Hello," Jack said. "I'm looking for a gentleman by the name of Douglas Gift."

"This is Douglas. But if this is a scam call, you can take my name off your list and then cram the list up your ass."

"No, sir, this is not a scam call. My name is Jack Rivers, and I am an agent with the Federal Bureau of Investigation. I'm calling to verify your identity. You're Douglas Gift of Buffalo, New York, correct?"

"I am," he said, clearly confused. "Wait…you said you're with the FBI?"

"That's right. Sir…you have a daughter named Rachel, correct?"

There was no response at first and then, after a few seconds, perhaps the most unexpected response of all. A rough bit of laughter. "I do. She in some sort of trouble?"

The absolute lack of emotion was disarming. Yes, he had a daughter and he hadn't sene her in forever. So what? Next question.

"No, sir," Jack said. "I'm a friend of hers. She has no idea I've made this call. But there are…well, there are things Rachel is dealing with right now and I think she may need to reach out to you at some point soon."

"Reach out to me?" Ah, there was a bit of emotion. Surprise and…was that sadness? "What for?"

"It's not my business to day."

"But you thought it was your business to make this call?"

"I did. I need to know straight from you that if she were to reach out and call you that you would accept."

This time, there was a thick silence from the other end. Finally, it ended, with: "Yeah. Yeah, you know, I think I might like that." There was another pause, and then: "Is she…well, how is she?"

"She's pretty amazing, Mr. Gift. Beyond that, I'll leave it to her."

"Yeah, okay," Douglas Gift saids, the words coming quickly.

"Goodbye," Jack said, ending the call.

Rachel had only mentioned her father a single time—a passing mention about how she wanted to patch things up with him before she died. Jack was quite sure it wouldn't have even been on her radar without the discovery of the tumor and the zero chance of surviving it, but she *had* mentioned it. And he felt that he had to do something for her. His thinking was that making that call—reaching out in any capacity—would be hard. So he thought if he ripped the Band-Aid off for her and started the ball rolling, it might be a big step forward.

Jack put his phone back into his pocket and wondered if he was overstepping. He had no idea what sort of rifts and history existed between Douglas and Rachel. And he also knew it was none of his business. But Rachel had been on his mind a lot lately. He wasn't naïve enough to misconstrue thoughts about her as romantic; she was a great agent and dependable friend, but she simply wasn't his type.

No, he was pretty sure the thoughts came from a part of him that understood how fleeting life could be. In a job where you carried a gun and were typically on the hunt for people breaking the law and ending lives, mortality often became a creature that stared you in the face with big, slobbering teeth on a daily basis. And now to have someone close to him staring that monster down every day, he couldn't help but feel for Rachel.

He left the bench and headed back inside. He hadn't seen Rachel today and figured he might swing by her desk to check in on her. He'd done his best to keep his distance when they weren't actively running cases together. She'd always seemed the type who preferred silence and isolation when facing something big.

As he neared the elevators just off the lobby, his phone rang. He was surprised at first, wondering if Douglas Gift had undergone a change of heart. Maybe hearing his daughter's name over the phone in such an unexpected way had simply shocked him and he'd responded by ending the call. But it wasn't until he reached into his pocket that he realized the phone that was ringing was not the personal phone he'd used to make the call, but the bureau cellphone in his left pocket.

Jesus, when did I become the pretentious a-hole that carries two phones on him? Jack wondered as he grabbed his work phone.

The number and extension on the display were familiar. It was Anderson. And Anderson usually only called when there was an unscheduled meeting being set up or if there was a case. He took the call while standing in front of the elevators, letting it pass by.

"This is Rivers."

"Agent Rivers, I need you to come to my office. I've got a case that just came in that I need you on. It's local, here in the city, and I'd like to have you headed to the crime scene as soon as possible."

"Sure, sir. What's the case?"

"All I know right now is it's a murder. And the victim seems to be connected to another body that was found a few days ago out near Brandermill. So come on up and I'll fill you in."

"Sure, sir. Want me to grab Rachel on my way?"

In an eerie resemblance to his conversation with Douglas, there was a brief silence on the other end of the line.

"Agent Gift is on a temporary leave of absence," Anderson said.

“She’s…what?”

“A leave of absence, for a period of at least two weeks.”

Jack wondered what this might mean. Had she finally told Anderson about her diagnosis? A wave of despair washed over him simply because he wasn’t quite sure what was going on. But he figured he’d not say anything about Rachel unless Anderson brought it up first.

“Rivers? Are you headed my way?” Anderson asked after a tense silence.

“Yes, sir. Be there in a few minutes.”

He ended the call, shocked and dumbfounded. A two-week leave of absence, and she hadn’t told him? It hurt a bit but beyond that, he found himself worried about her. Even as he pressed the button for the elevator, he wondered where she might be, and what she might be doing…and if he’d ever work with her again.

CHAPTER FIVE

The following day, Thursday, Paige Gift went back to school. She'd made the request without any prompting, though Rachel had offered her to take the rest of the week off. It was all guesswork, really. After all, how was she supposed to be able to predict how such a young child would handle the news that her mother would be dead in about a year? She figured it might be good for Paige to try to keep a sense of normalcy, so if she wanted to go back to school, who was she to question it?

So with Paige at school and Grandma Tate still occupying the guest bedroom, Rachel did her best to keep herself busy. She tidied up the living room. She dusted and vacuumed. The banal activities felt almost cathartic. Sure, there was a tumor in her brain but that didn't mean the dust was going to stop settling in around the house or that Paige was going to stop leaving her homemade slime and little bottles of glitter all around the house.

The act of cleaning was also something she'd often used in the past to focus her mind. As she swept and scrubbed, she thought of her two-week leave of absence and how it might affect the little bit of career time she had remaining. Was there really even any sense in going back? Beyond that, what about the Alex Lynch case? Was she supposed to be expected to just sit back and happily let someone else, some entire other arm of the government, track him down? She knew it seemed beyond conceited, but she felt that given her history with Lynch, she should have been the clear choice to lead the effort to hunt the man down.

She was vacuuming the carpet on the stairs when Grandma Tate appeared at the top of the stairway. She peered down with a look of grave concern, causing Rachel to shut the vacuum off.

"Something wrong?" Rachel asked.

"I just want to make sure you're not pushing yourself too hard."

Rachel bit back the sour reply that instantly came to her tongue—a reply about how Grandma Tate was being far too overbearing. Instead, she tried to keep things as pleasant but as firm as she could without causing a rift between them.

"I was working an active case as an FBI agent two weeks ago," she said. "I think vacuuming the stairs is going to be okay."

Grandma Tate furrowed her brow and sighed. "Don't forget who you're talking to, Rachel. I've been in your shoes. Hell, some days I feel like I still am. I know how it sneaks up on you. I'm just trying to watch out for you."

"I know you are."

And she did know how the wear and tear of her situation could sneak up on her. She'd experienced the blackouts, the thinning of her vision. She'd even crashed a car during the last case because of a moment of dizziness and confusion.

Still, there was something about Grandma Tate's watchful eye that was pissing her off. There was no sense in denying it. She did not regret having Grandma Tate come to stay with her and Paige, but it *was* starting to wear on her nerves.

"Tell you what," Rachel said. "I'm going to finish the stairs, make a little lunch, and maybe try to take a nap. Sound good?"

Her grandmother seemed to be confused on whether or not she was being made fun of but ended up nodding her head. She came down the stairs, sidestepping the vacuum cleaner. "I'll throw some lunch together. What do you want?"

Rachel waited to roll her eyes until Grandma Tate was behind her. And knowing that it was useless to argue, she said: "Just a ham and cheese sandwich, please."

She then turned the vacuum cleaner back on and finished the stairs. When she was done, she put the vacuum away and found her sandwich on the kitchen table, with a Granny Smith apple beside the plate. As for Grandma Tate, it seemed that she had walked out onto the back porch with her book of crossword puzzles. Rachel considered joining her just to catch a bit of sun, but decided against it. The nap she'd mentioned just to get her grandmother off of her back was starting to sound good. She didn't feel tired but she also knew she'd probably be able to doze off for a quick hour-long nap if she closed the door and turned the noisemaker on.

She sat down at the table with her sandwich and began to wonder if she'd made a mistake by being so unflinching with Anderson. What if she changed her mind next week and went back to him only to find that he'd taken offense to the way she'd reacted?

Really, in the grand scheme of things, she wasn't sure if it mattered. She had a very brief amount of time where she'd actually have to be concerned about what Anderson thought of her. It also made her wonder if she should just come clean with him, too. Everyone else close to her knew about her diagnosis so it was only a matter of time before he heard it, too.

She was roughly halfway through her sandwich when the doorbell rang. It was an odd sound to her, as it was rarely ever used. She wondered if it might be Peter, but could not think of a reason why he might come by in the middle of the day. Her thoughts then turned to Alex Lynch but she found it highly illogical that he'd be so bold as to come to her house—much less use the doorbell.

Still, she simply looked in the direction of the living room for several moments before getting up from the table. She decided to go ahead and answer the doorbell because if she didn't, another ring or two and there was a chance Grandma Tate would hear it and come rushing in to make sure she wasn't over-extending herself by answering the door. She left the remainder of her sandwich on the table, walked across the living room, and answered the door.

The person on the other side was not Peter or Lynch, but someone just as familiar as both. It was Jack, offering her a vague smile.

"Jack, how are you?" she said. At first, she was pleased to see him but then she remembered that she'd purposefully not told him about her decision to take a leave of absence if she could not get on the Lynch case. For all she knew, Jack might very well be pissed at her.

"I'm good, I suppose," he said.

"You mad at me?"

"Mad? No. But I'm a little concerned, and…well, can I just come in?"

"Of course." She opened the door and waved him in, closing the door behind him. She led him into the kitchen and sat back down to her sandwich. "Have you had lunch?"

"No, actually."

"There's leftover lasagna in the fridge if you'd like some. There's some tuna salad my grandmother made, too."

"I'll take you up on the tuna," he said.

"Help yourself." She waved absently at the fridge, trying to decide why Jack had made a surprise visit if it wasn't because he was angry at her for leaving work without telling him.

"So, a two-week leave of absence?" he said as he opened the fridge and found the right Tupperware.

"Well, the 'two weeks' part was Anderson's decision. I didn't put a cap on it."

"I know you didn't tell him about your tumor, so how did you explain it?"

"How do you know I didn't tell him?"

"Hey, I asked the question first." He popped the lid off of the tuna salad and then looked around, finding the loaf of bread on the end of the counter. He helped himself, plucking a spoon out of the silverware drawer (he found it without her help on the second guess) and layering the salad on a slice of bread.

"I asked him if I could be placed on the Alex Lynch case, and he said no. So I told him I wanted a leave of absence on the grounds that there was no way in hell I'd be able to focus on any other case if I knew Lynch was out there."

"Makes sense," Jack said, finishing the construction of his meager sandwich. "I guess he refused it because he thought the connection was just too personal?"

"Exactly. Now…answer *my* question. How can you know for sure I didn't tell him about the tumor?"

"Because he assigned me to a case and when I asked him if I could ping you on it, he told me about your leave of absence. And he asked me if I had any idea why you might have made such a decision other than Lynch. I, of course, said I couldn't think of anything. I think he needs to be told about your situation, but I'm not going to be the one to do it."

"I'm going to tell him. Maybe in two weeks."

"Hey, that's your decision," Jack said. He took a bite of his sandwich and sat down at the table with her. "But listen…that's not why I came here today. I came here to tell you about the case he assigned me to. It's got me worried…about you."

"How's that? What's the case?"

"Two people have been killed outside of medical facilities…cancer treatment centers. One was just off of Broad Street at the Colton Clinic. That one occurred late yesterday afternoon. The other happened in Brandermill three days ago, a fifty-seven-year-old male. Both victims had cancer, and they were terminal cases."

"You're certain that's the only thing linking the victims?"

"Right now, that's all we've got, yeah. And quite frankly, it's enough for me. You can call me overbearing and worrisome if you want, but I'm afraid you might end up being targeted."

She thought this over for a while and understood his concern. Two victims, both with terminal cancer…it was a pretty undeniable link. Still, to think she might be affected seemed like a bit of a stretch to her.

"You said both victims were attacked in parking lots, right?" she asked.

"Right."

"Well, I should be safe for at least another ten days. I don't have another appointment until then. And hopefully you'll have caught this guy by then. But…Jesus. Someone targeting people who already have a death sentence seems pretty grim. Who else is working it?"

"It just me for now, working with the police. I've got two interviews with family and friends lined up this afternoon, so that'll be fun."

"Is there a potential link to the doctors they're seeing, too?" Rachel asked.

"I checked into that. Nothing lines up. I've also looked at the specialists they were seeing beforehand as well. Nothing there, either."

"Well, how about—"

"Nope," Jack said, cutting her off. "Two weeks' leave. Remember?"

She scowled at him and shook her head. "Why did you come by here if it wasn't to pick my brain about it?"

"I came by to tell you about the specifics of the case and to ask you to please be careful. To watch your back, as it were."

"Well, I appreciate that. Thank you."

"You feeling okay?"

"I am. Maybe a tiny bit more tired than usual, but nothing bad."

"How's Paige handling it?"

"That's a tricky question. She understands what's going on but she's also trying to sort of pretend nothing is different for the most part. We may have to have a bigger conversation with her about it in the future."

"We?"

"Me and my grandmother." She hitched a thumb toward the back porch and said, "She's back there on the porch doing crosswords. Want to meet her?"

"I do love a good crossword," Jack said, getting to his feet. "But I have these interviews to get off to."

Rachel walked him to the door as he wolfed down the remainder of his sandwich. When he opened the door and stepped out, he remained there for a moment. It was clear that he wanted to say something else but couldn't find the words. There was something like sadness in his eyes when he finally spoke.

"You know, when this leave of absence is up and you're not…*better*…what does that mean? You and I won't be working together anymore, right?"

Rachel knew the answer was an almost definite *yes* but could not bring herself to admit it. So she tried to lighten the moment with a joke. "That depends on if you continue to come by my house to pick my brain during lunch."

He smiled and shook his head. "There's a tumor in your head, Gift. You keep making *pick my brain* comments and I'm not going to be able to take those freely offered puns."

"Understood. You be careful out there, Jack."

"Same to you."

He slowly walked away, but Rachel did not close the door right away. She watched Jack make his way to his car and, like him, wondered if their working relationship had come to an end and she hadn't even realized it until now. And if their working relationship was seeing its last days, what did that mean for them? What did that mean in regards to the efforts to bring in Lynch and any last hoorah she might be able to manage with her FBI career?

And if she let him go, what was she supposed to do? More chores? Sit around idly until Paige got home? Jesus…was that the life that was waiting for her if she let this damn tumor control her life from here on out?

Not me, she thought. *Nope, that's just not me.*

It all rushed by like wind strewn with debris, rushing across her brain and swirling her up in it like a miniature tornado. She made a decision in that moment that she *knew* was based on emotion rather than logic but was acting on it before she could take it back.

When she did close the door, a tear trickled down her cheek and she didn't bother wiping it away. What she did do, though, was turn back around and rush to the door. She did it without thinking, following her heart and her stronger impulses.

"Jack!" she yelled.

He was already at the car but when she called him, he wheeled around with a startled look on his face. "Yeah?"

"Give me a second, would you?"

"A second for what?"

"To speak with my grandmother," she said. "I'm coming with you."

"You're *what*?"

But she didn't bother answering. Instead, she ran to the back porch to tell Grandma Tate that she was leaving with her partner and might not be back for several hours.

CHAPTER SIX

"You're absolutely crazy, you know that?" Jack said from behind the steering wheel. "Or maybe I am. Maybe I'm the crazy one for letting you come along."

"Would you have tried to stop me, Jack?" she asked. "Really?"

"Maybe. I mean, Anderson is pretty upset about what you pulled yesterday."

"Am I being completely irresponsible if I suggest we just don't tell him I came along?"

The look of shock on his face surprised her. It was no longer a gentle back-and-forth ribbing of one another, but now treading on insubordination that could get them both in a bit of trouble.

"Yeah, maybe you are, a little. I just…I don't get it. Why would you request a leave of absence when you're clearly not ready for it? Was it just a powerplay against Anderson?"

"Maybe a little," she replied. She didn't see the point in lying about it. "I have limited time. I want to spend it in a way that's meaningful. And I had convinced myself that if I couldn't help bring Alex Lynch in, there was no point. But these terminal cancer patients…that hits a little close to home. I can't just sit idly by, you know?"

"So why not go directly to Anderson?"

She knew the answer but was ashamed to admit it out loud. She shrugged and looked to the floorboard, a clear indicator that she wasn't interested in answering. Jack understood this right away and let the issue lie. Still, Rachel could clearly see that the entire situation bothered him. It made her feel slightly selfish, thinking only of what *she'd* needed to keep her sanity and not how this might affect Jack's state of mind or, maybe even worse, his career.

"I'm glad to have you with me," Jack said, looking straight ahead into traffic. "But I need you to keep a backseat position on this. For your safety and my ass. Got it?"

He sounded both stern and compassionate and Rachel wasn't quite sure how to take it. As the state of his mood settled over her, she also realized that she was already feeling guilty for leaving Grandma Tate and Paige. It was a vicious circle that she was apparently never going to escape from, even when she wasn't *technically* on the job.

The remainder of the drive was quiet. It took a little over forty minutes to get to the crime scene, and when Jack pulled up to it, two things occurred to Rachel. First, he'd told her that he had interviews to conduct with family members of the deceased. Second, he'd insinuated that the most recent crime had happened "nearby." Neither of these seemed to be true, making her wonder if he'd secretly come by her house with the intention of getting her to come along the entire time.

When he pulled the car into the parking lot, Rachel gave him an accusatory stare. "I thought you said you had interviews to conduct."

He shrugged and offered a smile. "I lied. I wanted you to think that I was in the thick of it, really having to tackle this thing head on since I didn't have a partner."

"So I was supposed to feel guilty?"

"Hey," he said, parking the car. "I can't force you to feel any particular way."

"Ah, yet here I am."

Again, he only shrugged in a playful smart-ass way as they stepped out of the car. But when they were both out, he shook his head and something resembling sincerity passed across his face. "I thought you'd want in on this because of the topic…the characteristic of the victims. Call it poetic or just sappy, but it's almost like you're *supposed* to be on this one, you know?"

She said nothing, but she did understand what he meant. And in a very strange way, she appreciated the thought behind it.

They approached the scene together. Although there was no crime scene tape around the area within the lot where the victim had been killed, several of the parking spots around it had been cordoned off. Jack handed Rachel his phone and she saw that he already had some of the photos from the crime scene pulled up from before the body had been removed. She saw a young woman with prominent damage done to her head, sprawled out by a car.

"The victim was twenty-six-year-old Polly Warren," Jack said. "She was hit in the head twice from what we can tell, though the coroner may correct that. It's believed she was attacked after her afternoon appointment, pegging her as having died somewhere between five fifteen and five thirty-five—when another hospital visitor spotted her body on the pavement."

"Anything from forensics yet?"

"Nothing worth mentioning. Just before I arrived at your house, they found a bit of dirt on her pants but it turns out that came from right here in the parking lot."

"Have requests been put in for her medical records?"

"Yes, I did it myself last night. Of course, you know how that goes, though. Fortunately, we got lucky in that the next of kin was more than willing to help us out. A sister, I believe, who lives out in Poquoson. She confirmed that Polly had breast cancer, that it was in the late stages, and she was considered terminal."

Rachel stepped into the blocked off area and looked around the parking lot. As she studied the layout of the parking lot, she listened to Jack as he gave her more details. "When we tried finding anyone who passed by this area around the time we believed her to have been attacked, only one person was able to offer anything. It was a hospital employee, a janitor reporting for his late shift. He said he saw two people talking right here, right where she fell. He didn't see faces, but he did confirm that one appeared to be male, the other female. He also stated that there appeared to be no danger or animosity—that it looked like two friends were simply chatting."

"And I don't see cameras anywhere nearby," Rachel said. "The closest one is over there, to the left."

Jack looked in that direction, to where a small security camera was attached to the top of a light pole. "Yeah, and the police looked the footage over and there's nothing."

"And you said the first victim…the murder occurred in Brandermill."

"Yes. Want to head over there and take a look?"

"Have you already been?"

"I have," he said. "It's about as uneventful as this one."

"How about the coroner? Have you been there yet?"

"I haven't. It was on the list for today. But honestly, *whacked in the head* is still probably going to be the best we get. Still…want to head over there?"

Rachel thought it over for a moment. Paige would be home from school in about another hour and a half, and though Grandma Tate was more than happy to pick her up, there was still a great degree of guilt. Even Paige now understood that her diagnosis and limited time remaining was supposed to mean she'd be spending more time at home. So what would she think if her mother had already decided to change her mind about such things?

Well, it's a little late to worry about that now, she thought. *These are things you should have considered before leaving the house.*

Well, she was here now and supposed she may as well see it through. At least for today.

"Yeah, let's go. But let's make it quick. I'd like to try to be home before dinner."

"Sure," he said, already walking back to the car. He turned before opening the door, though, frowning. "Did I pressure you into this?"

"No. And I think it's adorable that you think you could pressure me into anything. It's just that…I don't want Paige to think I'm going back on a promise I told her."

"I understand. We better get going then."

When he got back into the car, Rachel could tell he was uncomfortable about the situation. But she knew Jack well enough; if she pressed him on it, he'd shut down. Maybe he'd be more willing to discuss it after another day or so. Or maybe she would just leave it alone. After all, she didn't see this being an issue beyond this case—a case she really had no business working on in the first place.

As it was now, they left the crime scene in silence and Jack drove them out toward the coroner's office. The silence was thick and heavy, and Rachel couldn't help but feel guilty that this was the atmosphere she'd created for what was essentially her last case…and her last time working as a partner with Jack.

***

Jack called ahead so when they arrived at the coroner's office, both bodies were already out and waiting for them. The coroner seemed to sense the strange mood hovering among Rachel and Jack, giving them access to the printed case files and then excusing himself. They stood in the large examination room together, looking over the bodies and the details.

The woman, Polly Warren, was on the examination table, as she was the most recent. But the other, a fifty-seven-year-old man named Benjamin Wells, was on a typical gurney, having been wheeled in from storage. Polly Warren looked to be in the worst shape, as her wounds had not yet been given the care and attention as Benjamin Wells's. Both had been killed in the same manner, with a series of blows to the head. There was only a single blow to Wells's head, directly cross the left temple, hard enough to cause the skull to cave in on that side. Polly Warren, however, had been hit twice—maybe three times. The two blows to her head were to the temple and just above the forehead. The potential third was just above her brow, but that particular wound might be the result of falling on her face on the pavement. There were scratches on her nose to also support this fact.

26

Rachel scanned the notes as she looked over each body. The notes were succinct and told the same story her eyes could see. There were no bruises or scratches anywhere other than the heads. The positioning of the blows indicated that they'd been facing their attacker when it happened. When Rachel put these factors together, she came up with a pretty clear picture of what happened: the killer had attacked while facing them, and neither victim showed any signs of a struggle or putting up a fight.

"Seems to me that the victim either knew the attacker or the attacker somehow lured them in under friendly pretenses," she said.

"Yeah, because if the attacks came from the front," Jack said, "it seems like he didn't sneak up or take them by surprise."

Rachel spent another five minutes looking the bodies over, scanning for anything else that might connect them—scars from surgeries, tattoos, anything. But she could tell fairly quickly that there was nothing. The only thing connecting them outside death was their terminal illnesses. And as far as Rachel was concerned, there was something beyond deplorable about that. Of course, maybe she was biased. She was, after all, in that same boat.

It made her wonder if the killer perhaps envisioned themselves as an angel of mercy, a means of shortening their painful and potentially dark final days. Perhaps the attacks were religious in nature, then, or maybe there was something much less tangible that she could not even conceive of just yet.

Still, looking at the bodies made her feel helpless in a way she rarely felt while examining victims. It went beyond feeling sympathy for them in that she, too, shared in their terminal illnesses. No, it was because as she looked to both of them knowing about that terrible link between them, it was far too easy to picture herself in their position.

This could be her very soon—and she wasn't nearly ready to face that yet.

"I want to talk to Polly Warren's family," Rachel said. "The sister from Poquoson. I assume she came to town after hearing about the murder."

"She did. She's currently staying with the brother." He sighed and said, "I figured you would want to talk to her. Looks like I'm not going to get out of speaking with an aggrieved family member after all."

Rachel knew he was just trying to make things a bit lighter—something he was usually pretty good at. But as they got back into the car, there was nothing light or remotely funny about what Rachel was

feeling. In fact, she couldn't remember the last time she'd ever felt so
lost.

CHAPTER SEVEN

Polly's brother lived just outside the town of Bottom's Bridge, in a house that was surrounded by overgrown grass and two junked trucks stacked up on cinderblocks. The house itself was quite nice, though. And when Jack knocked on the door, Rachel caught a whiff of roses coming from a flowerbed to the left-hand side of the porch.

The door was answered by a man who was clearly related to Polly. The resemblance was uncanny, right down to the piercing brown eyes. He regarded both with vague disinterest for a few seconds and then said, in a tired sigh: "Yeah?"

Rachel had to remind herself that this was technically Jack's case, so she made herself take the back seat. She remained quiet and stood to the side as Jack introduced them.

"I'm Agent Jack Rivers and this is my partner, Agent Gift. We'd like to ask you some questions about your sister, if that's okay."

He looked annoyed at once and made no attempt to hide it. "We already talked to the cops two different times," he said. "I'm not sure what else you're expecting to get out of us."

"Us?" Jack said. "So is your sister here?"

"She is. And she's a mess. So I don't see why talking about it over and ov—"

"Kevin, shup up and let them in," a haggard female voice called out from the back. Kevin rolled his eyes, shook his head, and opened the door wide. He did so in an exaggerated motion, as if making sure not only the agents, but anyone else who cared to come in, could enter.

Rachel and Jack walked inside, finding the house still and quiet. It had the feel of a place that had just been dealt bad news. It was a sort of stale feeling in the air that Rachel had long ago gotten accustomed to. The brother—Kevin, presumably—passed by them as they entered the living room and sat down in a well-worn armchair. At the same moment, a woman of about thirty or so stepped into the room through the adjoining kitchen.

"Is there new information?" this woman asked. The tired desperation in her eyes made Rachel badly want to be able to tell her that they *did* have some news for her.

"I'm sorry," Jack said, "but we don't. And I do understand that the cops have been by to speak with you," he added, looking over to Kevin. "But as the burau is now on the case, we'd like to ask some questions as well."

"Of course," the woman said.

"I take it you're the sister?" Rachel asked.

"I am. Melissa. I had been taking Polly to her chemo treatments at the start of it all. But she responded to the meds well and really didn't need the help. So I stopped. But I shouldn't have. I *know* I shouldn't have. If I'd been with her yesterday, this...this wouldn't have happened."

"You don't know that," Kevin snapped. He then looked to the agents and said, "Forgive her. She's wrecked and she tends to be a bit dramatic about things."

"Polly is *dead*," Melissa said. "You understand that, right?"

Kevin said nothing to this, electing instead to look at his fingers and pick at one of the nails.

"You said you were taking her to treatments," Jack said. "Did she insist you stop or was it something you decided on your own?"

"Oh, no, that was all Polly. She hated the idea that someone was going to wait on her. I live outside of town, and I was trying to arrange things where I'd be able to work remotely so I could be with her, sort of like a caregiver. But she wouldn't have that. And besides...she wasn't having any severe side effects from the chemo. Even the nurses and doctors said that after the first few doses, she'd likely be fine."

"Does that mean there was hope of remission?" Rachel asked.

"Well, I mean, I always held out hope. But the doctors were very upfront about the fact that it would take nothing short of miracle for her to fully beat it. Their best hope as of about a week ago was that she may be able to live another year and a half. The doctor she'd been seeing had mentioned two potential experimental procedures, one of which is starting to be utilized and working wonders in Sweden, but...but, no. I don't think remission was a real possibility."

"In terms of family members, is it just the two of you?" Jack asked.

"Just us," Kevin said dryly.

Wiping a tear away, only to be followed by another, Melissa said, "Yes, it's just us. Dad was never around and I have no idea where he even is. We haven't seen him for fifteen years or so. Mom died of breast cancer pretty early. No aunts or uncles...just us."

"Do either of you know if Polly was dating anyone?"

"If she was, she kept it a secret," Melissa said. "But really, I doubt she *was* seeing anyone. She's pretty lousy at keeping secrets."

"Any close friends she may have had a falling out with?" Rachel asked.

"I'm ashamed to say I don't know. She had friends, sure, but Polly always kept to herself. She was very much an introvert."

"Kevin, have you lived around here your whole life?" Jack asked.

"I have."

"So, within what? Twenty or thirty minutes of Polly?"

"That's right. But we rarely saw one another. We were never close. She'd call every now and then but that was about it."

"And when you learned she had cancer, you didn't offer to help in any way?"

Kevin didn't answer, though he was no longer staring at his fingers. In fact, he looked rather upset. He gave both agents a smirk and then got to his feet. He walked into the kitchen, where he opened the fridge and got out a beer. He sat at the bar area with his back to them and started drinking.

Melissa seemed heartbroken over his actions. She looked at him in both disgust and sadness and then back to the agents, as if embarrassed. "Kevin has been hurt for far too long," she whispered. "When Mom died, he changed. He shut down and closed himself off to everyone. And when he found out Polly had the very same cancer that killed our mother…he became hopeless. The most he's done is reach out to a local end of life foundation and got us set up to start the paperwork."

"End of life foundation?" Jack asked.

"Yeah, it's a non-profit that does what they can to help ease expenses on things like travel, bills, groceries, things like that. We'd just now started the paperwork and…well, I guess we won't be needing them now."

Rachel found herself looking over to Kevin, sitting in the kitchen. She knew that Melissa was probably right; he was hurting and simply dealing with it the best way he knew how. But there were also several signs of guilt present in the way he was behaving. It was almost like he might be hiding something.

Without looking away, she leaned over to Jack. "You good here for a second?"

"Yeah…" he said. She could tell that he was aware of what was on her mind and was not a fan of the idea.

"Excuse me, would you?" Rachel said to Melissa.

She got up and walked into the kitchen. She walked to the other side of the bar area rather than sitting in the stool next to Kevin. Standing across from him with the bar between them created a scene that was reminiscent of an interrogation room. She'd used this little trick before, knowing that it brought the person in question around to a more agreeable way of speaking. It subconsciously made them feel as if they were a subject of great interest rather than being questioned.

"You mind if I talk with you away from your sister?" she asked.

"I'd really rather not."

"You understand that we're only trying to help, right?"

"Of course I understand that. I just also understand that I am the very last person you'd want to be speaking with right now."

"And why is that?"

He allowed himself time to think by taking a long swallow from his beer. When he set it back down on the bar, Rachel saw emotion passing across his face. "Because it makes me seem like a monster when you hear the truth…the truth that I'm relieved she's dead. I'd rather have had her die like this, quickly and unexpectedly, than to have to suffer through her final days like our mother did."

"That doesn't make you a monster. If anything, I think there might be some sympathy buried inside such a sentiment."

"You'd be the only person to think so, if that's the case." He got to his feet, still holding his bottle of beer, and headed for the back door. "Please understand…I'm just not up to this right now."

He opened the back door and stepped out onto a small porch, closing the door gently behind him. Rachel remained where she was for a moment, letting what he'd said sink in. At its core, it was fairly suspicious, but there had been real hurt and pain in what he'd said. And if he was truly wrestling with such a thing, it made sense that he would not want to talk about it.

Going out in an unexpected blink as opposed to a slow, painful death, she thought. *Makes sense.*

More than that, given the last few months of her life, she also found that she could relate a little too well.

CHAPTER EIGHT

He sat in his darkened bedroom, looking at the computer screen. He'd set the glow to a low setting and even then, he had to tilt the laptop lid slightly downward so it did not shine directly on his face. He was looking at a Facebook profile for a man he'd never met. It was the profile of a man that was included on a list sitting to his right, the names obscured by the poor light in the room.

It had been quite easy to get the list—maybe too easy. It was just another indicator that he was doing the right thing. It almost seemed as if everything had been set up perfectly, the universe itself making sure he had everything he needed.

He'd only met with two people on the list, but things were moving along rather well so far.

It was also much easier than he'd expected.

He had assumed that taking the life of someone would be difficult—a gut-wrenching and heartbreaking endeavor that would haunt him. But he'd slept better than he had in ages ever since taking the first life, a middle-aged man with prostate cancer. In the man's final glimpse of the world of the living, there had been a flicker in his eyes— something that had looked very much like gratitude.

He was doing these people a favor. And what he'd seen in that man's eyes had proved that.

He'd not seen it in the woman's eyes. She had been far too confused in trying to determine if she had known him or not. But he had sensed a wave of relief coming over her when she'd fallen to the pavement. And in her final moments, he had no doubt that she'd been grateful to him. He'd spared her those last, awful months.

Feeling that he'd learend all about his next potential target that social media was going to give him, he closed the lid of the laptop and stepped out of his bedroom. His apartment beyond was small, tidy, and dark. His crimson-colored curtains were drawn tight, preventing any sunlight from getting in. Sunlight had been making him feel ill for a while now. Headaches, nausea, and these diamond-like sparkles that danced in front of his field of vision, making him feel dizzy.

He went into the living room and lay down on the couch. He had a television but he rarely watched it anymore. TV was a distraction, as was music and the job he'd quit three weeks ago. He had a nice little chunk of cash saved up and he figured when his *new* work was done, he could find another menial job and carry out the rest of his own miserable life.

Life. It was nothing but a ticking clock, a term and a set number of days that started counting down once an infant took its first breath. And from the moment that first breath was inhaled, the timer started and the process of death began.

It was his job to get those in pain to the escape of death quickly. Why allow the world and its troubles to taint their last days? He knew that most people frowned upon the idea of suicide, even when handed a terminal diagnosis. He was the answer for that; he was the quick and mostly easy way out of that tormenting decision and the difficulty that came with the little bit of life those poor, unfortunate people had to live.

He tried not to think too highly of himself. He was, after all, just a tool. He also knew a great deal about pain and suffering—as well as the desire to have life snatched away when in one's worst moments.

Almost absently, he reached over to the coffee table and looked at the list of people he'd been collecting. Yes, they were people with names, but he was more concerned with the names of the forces that were taking their lives. Prostate cancer, breast cancer, brain tumors, lung cancer, heart disease, AIDS. He focused on those factors because at the core of it all, those were the cause for death—not the people themselves. And focusing on those killers made it easier for him to take their lives.

Then, in the gloom on his apartment, he looked at their schedule of appointments, another handy feature of the list he'd managed to acquire. This was the most convenient thing of all, as it gave him a timeline as to when he would be free to attack. There was some planning and strategy to it if he did not want to get caught, but that had always been a strength of his.

If he did this right, he could be a savior of the terminally ill until he drew his last breath.

With a thin smile in the dark room, he thought: *Ah, and wouldn't that be poetic?*

He set the list and appointment schedule back on the table, already starting to focus on the next person he'd save and when he'd be doing it. And as luck would have it, it was very soon indeed.

CHAPTER NINE

When they arrived at the Wells residence to speak with the family of Benjamin Wells, Rachel found the exact opposite of what had been waiting for them at the home of Kevin Warren. Benjamin Wells lived in a well-spaced-out subdivision, the sort where each house had about two acres of land between their house and their neighbor. It was the sort of brick house that seemed to have taken over white-collar America in the 1980s; two stories with a pool in the back, but somehow not seeming all that glamorous.

There were five cars in the half-circle parking lot when they arrived. And when Jack knocked on the door, it was answered right away by two women who seemed polar opposites of one another. One of them greeted the agents with a smile while the other could barely hold eye contact with anyone, her eyes red and worn down from weeping.

"Can I help you?" the smiling woman said.

"We're Agents Rivers and Gift," Jack said, showing his badge. "We were hoping to speak to someone regarding Mr. Wells. A spouse, perhaps?"

"Of course, come on in."

As they walked through the door and Jack put his badge back inside his inner coat pocket, it occurred to Rachel that she was on a case without her badge or sidearm. It was a strange feeling that made the entire encounter feel more like a training exercise than a case.

"I'm Amy, Benjamin's niece," the smiling woman said. "His wife, Melinda, is in the den. I think she'd be up to speaking with you. But, as you could probably see from the little traffic jam in the driveway, she's got a lot of guests right now. Would you mind if I asked you to sit out on the sun porch? I'll send her right back to you."

"That's perfectly fine," Jack said.

"Cut through the kitchen, down the hall, and the door to the sun porch is right there at the end."

They followed these directions and found the sun porch easy enough. They stepped out on it and found a small lounger couch and a glider. It all looked out into the pool, which was still covered even though it had been warm enough to use it for a few months now. The porch had a cozy feel to it and the wear of the couch and the empty glass on the small coffee table indicated that it was used rather frequently. They both sat on the couch, leaving the glider for Mrs. Wells whenever she came out.

It took less than thirty seconds for the door to open and for the recently widowed Melinda Wells to come out onto the porch. The poor woman looked tired but also having just come out of the heavy-crying phase of having just learned her husband had been killed.

"Amy says you're with the FBI?" she asked, her voice soft and delicate.

"Yes ma'am," Jack said, again taking out his ID and showing it. "And we'll do our very best not to take up too much of your time."

Mrs. Wells settled into the glider and waved the comment away. "Oh, you take all the time you need. This will be a welcome change from hearing people tell me how my Ben is in a better place and such rubbish. He may very well be for all I know but…well, I want answers."

"We do, too," Rachel said.

"Mrs. Wells, the police reports show that the cops already asked you about any enemies your husband might have had and that you could come up with nothing. No business rivalries, no hardened friendships from the past…nothing. Have you been able to think of anything at all over the last few days?"

"No. Nothing at all."

"Can you tell us a bit about his cancer diagnosis?" Rachel asked. She had no real idea why but she found that she was almost afraid to hear the answer.

"He was diagnosed with prostate cancer seven months ago. He underwent chemo, saw a few specialists, and stayed in the hospital for a while. About eight weeks ago, it looked like he was going to beat it but then he took just an awful turn. The doctors told him it wasn't looking good—that even the chemo wasn't going to be of much help."

"The report also says that you were with him when it happened, right?" Jack said. "You were in the parking lot with him?"

"I was," she said. At this, she showed the first signs of true sadness. Rachel could see her fighting for control, her lips quivering and her breath shaky. "He was standing by the passenger's side door, waiting for me to unlock the doors. I was on the driver's side, digging the keys out of my purse. My head couldn't have been turned away for more than five seconds. But that was all it took. I heard the sound…something heavy hitting him. And by the time I looked up, he was falling."

"You never saw the attacker?"

"I caught sight of him as he was running away. He'd already managed to get a good distance away and was weaving in between the cars two rows ahead of us. I think…I think if I had called the police before going over to check on Ben, they might have caught him. But I was too worried. I wasn't thinking straight. Jesus…a good minute or two passed before I even thought about calling the cops."

"Did you see any part of the attacker that could be useful in trying to find him?"

"No. I know he was wearing a ball cap and a thin jacket—the sort that looks almost like a windbreaker but has more of an athletic fit about it. But that was all. No clue about age or height or hair color."

"And nothing was stolen?" Jack asked.

"No. This man killed my husband just for the sake of killing him," she said sternly. "It makes no damned sense."

"Did Mr. Wells have a cellphone he used regularly?" Rachel asked.

"He had one, but he only ever used it to FaceTime his daughter. And those damned crosswords he enjoyed so much." She smiled wanly and shook her head. "Our daughter is here, too, in the den. She's taken it quite hard. Hasn't spoken more than three sentences since she arrived. If you're curious about appointments, doctor's visits and things like that, I handled all of it."

"And everything had been going smoothly?" Jack asked.

"Yes. We even applied for some assistance through an end of life company and had been approved. I didn't even know such things existed, to be honest. We've always been financially well off but even with good insurance, this ordeal has sort of stripped us."

"What can you tell us about this company?" Rachel asked. Melissa Warren had also mentioned reaching out to an end of life foundation for assistance with Polly. It would be a strange link, but a link all the same.

"Well, they call themselves a foundation, actually. They're supposed to be able to relieve us of burdens like groceries, traveling to and from the doctor, any in-home care we need. That sort of thing."

"What are they called?"

"Life Fulfilled. They seem to be a very nice group. They're a non-profit that I read nothing but good things about."

"Mrs. Wells, do you think—" Jack began. But he was interrupted by a loud, piercing wail from elsewhere in the house.

Rachel got to her feet at once, instantly reaching for a sidearm that wasn't there. But within another second, she understood that it wasn't a scream of alarm, but one of unhindered grief.

Mrs. Wells got to her feet, her hand going to her heart. "That's my daughter. She…I've known this was coming. I'm sorry…I have to go…"

"Of course," Jack said. "Thank you for your time."

Mrs. Wells left the sun porch, hurrying back down the small hallway. As she did, her daughter's wails became heartfelt screams, pleas for her father. *"I want to see him! Someone take me to seeee hiiim!"*

It broke Rachel's heart to hear it. They made their way quickly out of the house but even as they excused themselves back outside, they could hear the screams of the daughter. When they were off of the porch, Rachel found herself nearly sprinting to the car because it was far too easy to layer the moment over her own life—that she was the deceased and the screams were coming from Paige.

Paige, she thought. *You know she'll be home in about half an hour, right? Don't you think it's time you get back home? Don't you think it's time to finally make her a priority?*

She did, and she wanted very badly to voice it. Instead, she vowed that she would make it a point to be home to tuck her daughter into bed. But even that felt like a tear in her heart because this case was already feeling far too personal to her—almost as if she were being targeted and taunted over it.

Instead of dwelling on the work-versus-home struggle, Rachel sat down in the passenger seat and gave Jack a determined stare. "So…Life Fulfilled. I think if it's the same foundation Melissa Warren mentioned, it's got to be checked out."

"I'll make a call and find out," he said. "You want to do some Google-Fu to see what you can find on the place?"

She pulled out her phone and typed in the name. The website she found for Life Fulfilled gave a very succinct picture of what the foundation did. As she read over the details, Rachel discovered that it was more or less the equivalent of what the Make-A-Wish Foundation was for children. It was a non-profit that did what they could to make the final days of people with terminal illnesses as enjoyable as possible. In some cases, it was exactly as Melissa Warren and Mrs. Wells had described—a way to help relieve financial and time burdens. But in some cases, they worked to help the ill achieve dreams or goals that their suddenly-shortened lifespan would not allow otherwise. They were located in Richmond and their website encouraged people to drop by for a visit if they were in need of such services.

As she looked over the website, she also listened in on Jack's call. He was looking for a specific officer—presumably whoever he'd been working with over the past day or so. He was bounced around a few times before he finally got the officer he needed.

"I spoke with Melissa Warren today," he said. "Yes, Polly's sister. She mentioned an end of life foundation that they'd been working with. Do you have any information on that?" A pause and then, "Yeah, sure. Okay. And what's the name?" He looked to Rachel and nodded as he said, "Life Fulfilled. Perfect. Thanks for your help."

He ended the call and waited a moment, as if he was expecting her to say something.

"What?" Rachel asked.

"You need to call it a day?"

"Sort of. But this seems like a solid link. And if it's relatively close and on the way home, I don't see the harm in visiting."

"You sure?"

No, she thought. *No, I want to be with my daughter and I can't for the life of me understand why I'm having such a difficult time turning away from work.*

"I'm sure. But I think that may end up being the end of my little excursion for the day."

He opened his mouth and then closed it quickly. She was pretty sure he'd almost asked once again if she was sure. Instead, he nodded and started the car. And when they pulled away from the house, Rachel wondered if it was only her imagination or if she truly could still hear Benjamin Wells's daughter screaming.

CHAPTER TEN

The offices at Life Fulfilled did a good job of camouflaging the sort of business they did. The place gave off the feel of a travel agency rather than a foundation that worked with the sick and dying. It started with the colorful yet simple logo on the door and continued with the cheerful woman sitting at the front desk. Behind her, large pictures of people engaging in a variety of activities hung on the wall: playing chess, lounging on the beach, sitting on a ski lift.

"Can I help you?" the woman at the desk asked.

"Maybe," Jack said, again showing his badge. "We're Agents Rivers and Gift, with the FBI. We're looking into a pair of murders and have recently discovered that both victims have applied for assistance here."

"Oh my goodness," the woman said, shocked. Rachel noticed that she was at a legitimate loss for words as she tried to think of what to say next. "Were they…they had gotten in contact with us?"

"Yes, and we believe one of them applied recently," Rachel said. "Would the manager happen to be in?"

"No, I'm sorry. He's at a conference in New York. He should be back tomorrow, though. I'm sure we can set up a meeting."

"We may need to do that," Jack said.

"Is there anything I can help you with?"

"Could you confirm for us that you've received applications from Benjamin Wells and Polly Warren?"

The woman seemed torn over this and, after a handful of seconds, shook her head in deep regret. "I'm so sorry. I really can't do that. But my boss, the foundation chairman and manager Wes Dalton, can. Really, I think you'd need to speak with him."

"Totally understood," Jack said. "Would you mind if we had a look around?"

"Oh, help yourself." She stood up from her chair, all too eager to please after having to deny them the client information. "If you want, I can give you a quick tour—though it isn't much, really."

She was right. Beyond the lobby at the entrance, there was only a small hallway with three rooms—two on the left and one larger one on the right. It was all very minimalist in nature, with glossy wood floors and beige walls with large framed pictures similar to the ones behind the front desk.

"I assume you're aware of the assistance and services we provide?" the receptionist asked.

"To an extent," Jack said. "Would you say the majority of your clients fall into the wish-list category or the financial assistance and help category?"

"Oh, the assistance, by far. It's odd, but it almost seems as if the loved ones that typically call us and do most of the paperwork are almost embarrassed to ask for help. So far, already eight months into the year, we've only had three clients request something special; one of those was for help in planning and paying for a three-day trip to Disney World for their sick daughter."

She had lowered her voice a bit near the end of her answer. As they passed by one of the rooms, Rachel could see that a meeting was taking place. There were doors to the little meeting rooms, but they were all open. In the room she was looking into, a Life Fulfilled employee was sitting on one side of the table while an older gentleman and a young woman sat on the other side.

The receptionist pulled them quickly into another room, the next one down on the left side. "So, for instance," she said, "the meeting taking place that you just saw is for a man suffering from heart disease. His daughter has expressed to us that one of his longtime dreams is to go to a Baltimore Ravens game. We've told her that we can get her pretty much any seats she wants. A single call and he's sitting on the fifty-yard line. But she's hesitant because she feels that *she* should be able to afford it herself. Even when people are on the brink of death, most find it very hard to ask for help."

"How many clients do you typically have at one time?" Rachel asked. She was aware that hearing about the services was almost like having someone talk about her behind her back while she was in another room. Hearing about people close to death due to terminal illnesses while she was dealing with her own was surreal and a little painful.

"Well, right now, we are working with eleven. And we do our best not to ever have more than twelve. With the small staff here, it's a bit difficult to manage more than that. We have a waiting list of about eight or nine people at the moment and when Mr. Dalton gets back, we'll be discussing who we can bring on from that waiting list now that we have that one single opening."

Rachel was already sensing that their time here was coming to an end. There was nothing to help them here currently—not until Wes Dalton returned from his trip to New York.

"When will Mr. Dalton be returning?" she asked.

"We don't know, actually. It may be tomorrow afternoon, but it could be as late as lunchtime or so the following day."

Jack dug out his wallet and plucked out a business card. He handed it over to her and said, "Would you please have him call us when he returns. We'd really like to see if we can get more information on our two victims."

"Of course. And again…I'm very sorry I couldn't help. We have very specific instructions not to hand over client information."

"It's okay," Jack said. "We understand. Thanks for your time."

They made their way out of the office, stepping back out onto the street. When they were back in the car, Jack started the engine but didn't pull off right away. "Is this weird for you?" he asked. "Having to hear about these people planning for the end when you…well, when you…you know…"

"It's a little strange, yeah. But it's also making me want to do what I can to catch this creep."

"I figured. Seems you may have asked Anderson for your leave of absence a little early, huh?"

"Yeah, and—"

Rachel's phone rang and even though she knew it was coming from Grandma Tate thanks to the caller display, she still nearly answered it *"Agent Gift."* She supposed it was just her natural instinct whenever she was with Jack.

"I need to get this," she said. Jack nodded and started scrolling through his own phone as Rachel answered. Rather than answer formally, she answered with: "I know. I should have been home by now."

"Well, that's according to what you told me," Grandma Tate said. "But honestly, it's no big deal. Paige got invited to one of her friends' house for the afternoon. A little girl name Suzanne. You know her?"

"Yes, and I know her mother, too," Rachel said. She felt relief at first—in that she now had an out to remain with Jack and the case for a bit longer—and then guilt for feeling that way. "If you're fine with it, I am, too."

"She says it's just two blocks or so over, is that right?"

"It is, yes."

"Then I think I'll just walk her over. Do you think you'll be home in time for dinner?"

She almost answered yes right away, but didn't want to paint herself into another lie. She answered as honestly as she could with: "I just don't know yet. I'll certainly be home before Paige has to go to bed, though."

There was the slightest hesitation from the other end of the line and Rachel didn't blame her. Grandma Tate was likely annoyed, maybe even a little disappointed. "That's fine. I believe we'll just have one of those oven pizzas for dinner."

Rachel heard this, but she also watched as two people exited the Life Fulfilled offices. It was the older gentleman and his woman companion. Now that she saw their faces, she was quite sure they were father and daughter.

"That sounds good," Rachel said, her attention now on the father-daughter pair. "Thanks again for this."

"I'm just happy to do what I can. But…if you don't mind my saying so, you really need to hang it up soon."

"I know." But even then, she was already reaching for the door handle to step outside. "I'm trying. I'm still figuring things out."

"I know, dear. Now, you get back to whatever it is you're doing. Paige and I will be fine."

As they ended the call, Jack looked to her, realizing that she was getting out of the car. Before he could ask what, exactly, she was doing, Rachel walked quickly over to the older man and his daughter. She wasn't quite sure what she wanted to say to them, but she did feel getting an insider view of how Life Fulfilled worked would be important to the case.

"Excuse me," she said, catching up to the pair as they made their way to a small truck parked along the side of the curb. "Excuse me, sir?"

They both turned to her and she was surprised to see that the younger woman looked relatively happy. Apparently, the meeting they'd just had was a good one. The older gentleman looked tired but there was the trace of a smile on his face as well.

"Yeah?" he said.

"I'm Agent Rachel Gift, with the FBI." She said this, realizing she had no ID. But Jack was there, coming in behind her and showing his badge. It was yet another thing that made her feel like she was really nothing more than a supporting actor.

"And I'm Agent Rivers," he said.

"We're looking into a few things for a case in the area," Rachel said. "And Life Fulfilled came up. Now, we don't necessarily suspect them of anything, but we're trying to get a better understanding of how they operate. Would you be willing to share your experience?"

The father looked to the daughter, as if for permission. "Yeah," he said. "I think that would be okay."

"I don't see why not," the daughter said. "Now, you said there's nothing going on with them, right?"

"Nothing that would raise alarms, no," Jack said. "It's more about them being referenced in a case."

"Oh...well, I have nothing but good things to say about them," the daughter said. She smiled again, her face lighting up. She was very pretty, her blue eyes the same as her father's. Rachel suspected the blonde hair had also come from her father, though the bit of hair he did still have remaining was thin and gray.

"They're maybe a little *too* kind," the father said.

"And they're a non-profit, so I'm still not sure where all the money comes from," the daughter said. "They've told us that if we want, Dad can get just about any seat for a Ravens game in Baltimore. They're even willing to have someone drive us."

"And was this something you asked for specifically?" Rachel asked.

"No. But during the first meeting we had with them, they'd asked about things he now feared he wouldn't be able to do because of what is looking to be a shortened lifespan. He mentioned never getting to go to a Ravens game and they sort of zoned in on that. It's probably because he really never asks for anything. Now, we're only on the waiting list for right now, but they're already trying to make plans for us."

"Do you mind me asking what you've been diagnosed with?"

"Severe rheumatic heart disease," the father said with a practiced sort of irritation. "I'm on enough meds where it's bearable but there's no long-term solution. Eventually, it's going to kill me."

"Dad..."

He shrugged and offered Rachel a smile. "Football season starts in two weeks. I may have the full length of the seasons...maybe even all the way to the Super Bowl. But seeing as how the Ravens sure as hell won't make it to the Bowl, I think maybe I'm going to take them up on those tickets."

Rachel nodded and only continued looking at them out of respect. Hearing him talk so openly and honestly about his condition made her want to cry. He'd accepted the hand he'd been dealt and was to the point that he could off-handedly mention it without getting emotional. He almost seemed hopeful, despite his condition. She almost envied him.

"Thank you for your time," she said. "And I certainly wish you the best."

She hurried back to the car and basically fell into the passenger's seat. When Jack was once again behind the wheel, he made a point to look her in the eyes—something he typically didn't do.

"I think maybe you need to call it a day. I see now that it was a mistake to bring you along."

"Maybe it was. But I have to see it through."

"Then I have to tell Anderson you're coming with me. This is going to get me in a heap of shit if he finds out."

"Then we'll be careful."

He sighed and looked out to the streets. "Okay, then. The waiting list. I feel like that's the next move. If both Wells and Warren were on the waiting list—"

"Then the killer may have a copy and is using it," she finished for him. "He may also be on the list, knocking off people so he can get to the top faster."

"Grim, but yeah…that's what I'm thinking."

"It's just a matter of getting it."

Jack looked back to the Life Fulfilled offices, considering something. As an idea came to him, he started to slowly nod his head. "Stay here one second."

"What are you—"

"I'll be right back."

He got out of the car and went hurrying back to the building. She watched him slip inside and, through the picture window along the front, she saw his blurred shape speaking to the woman behind the desk. She knew he could be charming when a situation called for it; it was a talent she often ribbed him for but had turned out to be useful on more than one occasion.

As she waited for him to come back, she watched the father and daughter pull away, back out onto the street. She thought of the hard stretch of time the daughter would be facing in the next six months or so—the pain, the loss, the grief. More than that, though, she thought of the old man, knowing that death was right on his heels and living his life the way he chose anyway.

Maybe that was what she was doing. Maybe her refusal to truly put her career as an agent behind her was because it meant more to her than she thought. Grandstanding and telling Anderson that she wanted her leave of absence suddenly seemed like not only a bad idea but an early defeat.

But Paige…

She had to admit to herself that Paige was the only reason she had to quit. If there was no Paige, she could easily see herself chasing down criminals until she could literally no longer walk.

Yeah? some wiser part of her spoke up. *And how many more cars would you end up crashing during your last cases? How many more times would you be willing to put Jack's life in danger?*

She'd been so wrapped up in her thoughts that she didn't see Jack coming back to the car. When he opened the driver's side door, she jumped in surprise. He showed her his phone as he slid his seatbelt on.

"Looks like I've still got it," he said.

Rachel looked to the phone and saw a list of names and telephone numbers. On it, she saw the names Benjamin Wells and Polly Warren. "How'd you get it?"

"I very politely asked the lady at the desk to see if she could get her manager on the phone—that it could very well be a matter of life and death for someone. She did, and I spoke with him. He gave her immediate permission to send me a copy."

"Damn good work, Rivers. So…you know what we might have here, right?"

"A potential list of victims," he said. "And maybe even the name and contact information of our killer."

CHAPTER ELEVEN

Rachel stared at the Life Fulfilled wait list as Jack took a moment to hit a drive-through for an early dinner. While it did her a great deal of good to see both of the names there, thus solidifying the link, there was one thing that bothered her.

"Both Warren and Wells aren't anywhere near the top of this," she said. "Twenty-one names, and Wells was number seventeen. Warren was number twelve."

"I thought the same thing," Jack said as he took the slightly greasy bag of food from the person at the window. "But for a list like this, I doubt freeing a spot up means someone else instantly fills that slot, in that order. That's the impression I got when I spoke to Wes Dalton, anyway."

"Okay, so maybe the killer is someone beneath Wells…someone who's just trying to work their way up the list any way they can," Rachel suggested. "One off the list, no matter how low down on the list they may be, means the killer gets moved up a position."

"Makes sense, I suppose," Jack said. "And if he's choosing them randomly, that's going to make things a bit harder on our end."

"And that's *if* he's getting the names of these people off of this list. There's a similar chance he may have somehow gotten the names from the doctors' offices Wells and Warren were visiting. So we may need to eventually speak to the employees at those offices."

"You know, I can't help but notice that you keep saying *we*," Jack said. "As if you're part of this case on an official basis."

"So I'm just along for the ride?" she asked with a smirk. "Is that what you're saying?"

"If it happens to come up with Anderson, yes. Actually, I may even say you coerced or bullied me."

"Well, then if I'm just along for the ride, why don't *you* call the office and see if you can get addresses to go with these names and numbers beneath Wells?"

Unwrapping his burger, he said, "Sorry, I'm eating."

"Yeah, but you—"

Her words froze up for a moment as an enormous wave of vertigo swept through her. It came out of absolutely nowhere, causing her to lean to the right against the door. She closed her eyes but even then, she could feel it. It wasn't too dissimilar from being drunk, lying down on a bed and closing her eyes, waiting for the world to recenter itself.

The disorientation was accompanied by a very faint throbbing sensation along the back of her head. It did not hurt, but felt more like a slightly pulled muscle. She reached up to massage the area but was so dizzy that her hand missed the back of her head. It felt like she was swimming, doing a backstroke.

"Rachel?"

She took a second to respond to Jack, not sure if she even trusted herself to speak in that moment. Her first rection, of course, was to assume this was related to the tumor. If it was, it was a new symptom. But it was already beginning to pass. And while this was a relief, she knew better than to assume it was gone for good.

"Rachel. Are you okay?"

"Yeah. Just got a little light-headed for a second."

"You okay?"

She nodded, finally opening her eyes. Things were a little swimmy, but much better than they had been as recently as five seconds ago. "Yeah, I think so."

"Maybe I need to take you home."

"No, I think I'm good. Let's at least see what we can find out about the people below Wells on the waiting list. You have my word that I'll let you know if I start to feel off."

He took a bite of his burger, shaking his head at her. "If you die while shadowing me on this case you haven't even officially been assigned to—"

"I promise, I won't die. Not from the tumor, anyway. But you talking to me with a mouthful of food might do it."

"Smart ass."

Rachel smiled at him as he drove with his free hand, shoveling more burger in with the other.

***

They started at the very bottom of the list and got an address for a woman named Elizabeth Foster. She lived just off of Broad Street, only a fifteen-minute drive from where Jack had gotten his greasy burger. It was a quaint brownstone, with well-cared-for azaleas lining the sidewalk.

Rachel knocked on the door and it was answered by a younger woman. She was dressed in a plain white T-shirt and loose-fitting khaki shorts. Her hair was done up in a ponytail, and there was a slight sheen of sweat on her forehead. She smiled in a practiced and tired sort of way as she greeted them.

"Yes? Can I help you?"

Rachel took the lead, showing her badge and making introductions. "Agents Gift and Rivers," she said. "We were hoping to speak with Elizabeth Foster. Are you a family member?"

"Oh, no, I'm Mrs. Foster's caretaker. Jasmine O'Toole."

"Is Mrs. Foster currently in?" Rachel asked. "We have some questions to ask her regarding Life Fulfilled and the process of getting on their list."

"Well, I do know that she's napping right now and between the three of us, I'd really prefer not to wake her. However, if you're wanting to know about those specific things, I could help you. I sort of took over during that entire process." She frowned a bit and gave them a soft, skeptical look. "Is that why you're here? To talk about that whole mess?"

Jack grinned and said, "Well, it wasn't. But if there was a mess of some kind, maybe we should hear about it."

Jasmine nodded in understanding and stepped to the side to allow them in. She led them through a foyer that looked like something out of a *Better Homes and Gardens* magazine. There were plants in every available space, a cute coat rack, and an umbrella stand. The foyer flawlessly transitioned into a short hallway that emptied out into a den. Before they entered the den, a large kitchen opened up on the right and it was there that Jasmine led them.

"Can I get you some coffee or tea?" she asked.

"Coffee would be fantastic," Jack said.

"Same for me," Rachel said.

As Jasmine took mugs down and poured coffee from an expensive-looking coffee maker, Rachel got to the point. "To start off, we should tell you that the case we are working on may very well be related to the Life Fulfilled waiting list. Over the past few days, there have been two murders in the area and we've recently discovered that they were both names on that list."

Jasmine paused mid-pour on the second mug. "Oh my goodness," she said. "That's awful." She continued to fill the mug, a sour look on her face as a result of the news.

"Now, it's just a working theory, but we can't help but wonder if this murderer might be trying to shorten the waiting list for his own benefit. So we're checking in on recent applicants for Life Fulfilled services."

"However," Jack said, "you mentioned a mess of some kind. What was that about?"

Jasmine brought over the coffees, bringing a small decorative bowl of sugar over as well. "Well, I wasn't directly involved in it," she said as she went to the fridge and got out a small bottle of creamer. "It was Mrs. Foster's son, Charlie."

"So what happened, exactly?" Rachel asked as she started doctoring up her coffee.

"From the way Mrs. Foster and a few folks down at the Life Fulfilled offices explain it, Charlie had no idea there would be a waiting list. He'd learned about their services online. He filled out the initial application and got a call within a few days. From what I was told, the face-to-face interview went remarkably well…until right at the end when they told him Mrs. Foster would be placed on their waiting list. At that point, he lost it. According to Mrs. Foster, it had been coming for a while. Taking care of her for so long and being fearful that she was going to die ate away at him. And right there in those offices, he just snapped."

"Snapped how?" Jack asked.

"That depends on who you ask," Jasmine said. "Mrs. Foster tells me that Charlie got to his feet and screamed a bit. He used some foul language and then walked out, pushing her right along in her wheelchair."

"But Life Fulfilled has another version?" Rachel said.

"Yes. I've spoken with the manager and the woman who oversaw the face-to-face interview. They both say Charlie threw a chair and threatened to beat the brains out of the woman giving the interview—Beth Gantry, I think her name is. It got so heated that they called the police."

"How long ago was this?" Rachel asked.

"Maybe two months…give or take a few days."

"Were you working for Mrs. Foster at that time?"

"Not yet. I'd interviewed with Charlie and had gotten a call-back. I suppose you could say I was in sort of a training period when this all happened."

"Were you surprised when you heard about the outburst?" Rachel asked. "Had you ever seen anything in him that made you think he might be prone to those kinds of actions?"

"I caught little glimmers of frustration here and there whenever he'd talk about the cost of medicine or how the insurance process was a bit too much, but nothing over the top."

"I take it you got the job, correct?" Jack asked.

"I did."

"And how often does Charlie come around?"

"Not nearly as often as he used to. Once things fell apart with Life Fulfilled, there seemed to be some strain and tension between him and his mother. She says there were a few days where she heard him on the phone, trying to apologize to them but then demanding they put her higher up on the list." As she said this, Jasmine seemed to understand what all of this might mean. Her eyes trailed off to the side as she seemed to consider it all for the first time.

"When is the last time you saw him?" Rachel asked.

Jasmine took a moment to think it over, sipping absently from her own cup of coffee. "Ten days ago, I guess it was. Maybe eleven. He came by to check on her and they watched *Jeopardy* back in her bedroom. He didn't say a word to me. He just left."

"And what about Mrs. Foster?" Rachel asked. "What's her diagnosis?"

"Breast cancer. The chemo was brutal on her, but the doctors have seen some improvement. She'll never….well, she'll never actually beat it, but they think she's going to make several years beyond what they'd originally thought."

"What was the end result with Life Fulfilled?"

"Well, they took her off of the list for a while, but I pleaded with them a few weeks ago. They put her back on, and we know she's way down on the list. But even if it takes a year…anything they can offer is going to be amazing."

"Jasmine, would you happen to know where Charlie lives?" Rachel asked.

"I've never been there personally, but yes. I've got it on an envelope around here somewhere if you want me to hunt it down."

"He's local?" Rachel asked.

"Yeah, over in Midlothian somewhere. But…I really don't think he…I mean, I'd be very surprised if he had it in him to actually murder anyone."

"I'm not sure we're quite jumping to that conclusion," Rachel said, though she wasn't quite so certain. She took another long sip of her coffee and nodded to Jasmine with a smile. "Thanks for your time…and the coffee."

"Also," Jack said, reaching into his inner coat pocket and pulling out a business card. "When Mrs. Foster wakes up, please let her know we stopped by. Just in case she can think of anything else that may help us."

"Of course."

Jasmine walked them back through the house and opened the front door for them. Rachel thought she could sense a severe shift in the woman's attitude—a stark difference from the smiling, bright woman who had greeted them.

"I do apologize if this bit of news has you upset or frightened," she said. "Please feel free to use that card if you think you may be in danger of any kind. Keep the door locked and maybe just be a bit more aware over the next few days."

"Yeah, I will be," Jasmine said. "Thanks for stopping by."

Rachel and Jack returned to their car, Jack making sure to take the wheel. "God, I hate to spook that poor woman like that," Rachel said.

"I think she appreciated the honesty, though," Jack said. He'd pulled out his phone and scrolled to a number. Rachel didn't have to ask what he was doing; they'd worked together long enough for her to know the next step. He was calling up the records department back at the field office, looking to see if there were any red flags on Charlie Foster.

With the call placed, he set it to speaker mode and handed it to Rachel. She had to remember that she technically wasn't even supposed to be there, making sure to keep quiet as the other line started ringing.

A somewhat familiar male voice answered the phone, tired and seemingly excited to get any sort of call. "This is Monty, with records."

"Monty, it's Jack Rivers. Can you run a criminal report for me?"

"Yeah, sure thing." Rachel could hear the light pattering of fingers across keys and then Monty said: "What's the name?"

"Charlie Foster," Jack said. "Should be a current address listed as somewhere in the Midlothian area."

"One second." Again, the sound of keys being typed clattered through the phone. Rachel wondered what it said about her that she found the noise rather pleasant. Ten seconds or so passed, and Monty's voice came back over the phone. "Charlie F. Foster, born March 8, 1981. I've got two assault charges and one count of harassment."

"How recent?" Jack asked.

"Nothing any more recent than two years ago. But the assault charges came within just a few months of one another. Both filed by the same person…a woman listed at the time as his wife. The harassment charge is from five years back, filed by someone named Mark Scotts. Hold on…" A few clicks, and then he was back again. "It took place at a minor league baseball game. The police report says he started a fight when he was harassing a man about allegedly talking on his phone through the entire game."

Rachel tried not to get too excited. They were red flags for sure, and it did line up with the behavior that took place at the Life Fulfilled offices. But it was far from a smoking gun. On the other hand, it was more than enough to warrant him a visit.

"What's the address?"

As Monty recited it, Rachel tapped it into her own phone, pulling it up on her maps app.

"Thanks, Monty," Jack said. "Gotta run."

He pulled the car away from the Foster house and looked over to Rachel. She knew the look and, before she even knew she was doing it, shook her head.

"Nope."

"Nope what?"

"Nope, I don't need to go home yet. Paige is on a play date. As long as I'm home by the time she gets to bed, I'll be fine."

"You're pushing it, Gift," he said, eyeing her with mock irritation. Only…*was* it mockery? Or was her insistence on being involved on this case truly starting to get under his skin?

Well, he should have thought of that before he came to my house, she thought.

With that growing tension between them, Jack pointed the car west and headed to the residence of their first real lead.

CHAPTER TWELVE

Jack was beginning to regret that he'd gone to see Rachel. He'd not been naïve about it. He'd known she would want to come with him and he'd been fully prepared to allow her to come to the crime scene to have a look and offer some opinions and insights. But he'd been sure it would stop there. With the way the last case had gone and after putting in her request for a temporary leave of absence, he didn't see why she'd want to press on any further.

So as he parked the car in front of the small suburban home of Charlie Foster, Jack had to admit it to himself: this was his fault. While he could simply put his foot down and demand that she shut up and let him take her home, he couldn't bring himself to do it.

He was starting to realize that she needed the job. He knew she loved Paige more than anything in the world, but he also knew that in order to keep her mind sharp and sane, she needed her work. He almost pitied her for having to manage that balance in her current predicament. Yet at the same time, he knew he could be heavily reprimanded if Anderson found out she was with him.

Before opening the car door, Jack looked over to her. He could tell her mind was brimming with thoughts—maybe trying to operate that balance he'd just thought of, or maybe figuring out how to take back her request for a leave of absence without it coming off as wishy-washy and unprofessional.

"I need you to think about the logistics of this," he said. "It's been almost four hours and it's getting to be night. As your partner and friend, I'm going to strongly urge you to go back home after this. We're risking too much. Your health, my job security. You understand that Anderson would go nuclear if he knew you were with me while you're technically on leave, right?"

"I know."

"Besides, I'm driving. You have to go where I take you, right? And after this—after we speak with Charlie Foster—I need to take you home for both our sakes."

He could tell that she wanted to argue but fought it. Her lips pressed together tightly as she nodded her head. "That's fair," she said, but it was clear that she wasn't entirely convinced. "But would you keep me in the loop on this? I feel…I don't know…*connected*? Killing these terminally sick people…it's hitting harder than I thought."

"I can promise to do my best to keep you up to date. How's that?"

"So long as you keep your word."

"Do you regret putting in for the leave of absence?"

Rachel simply gave a shrug and opened the passenger's side door. "I don't know just yet."

They walked together up a thin sidewalk that led to Charlie Foster's house. He lived on the backside of a suburb in a house that looked identical to all of the others on his block. It wasn't an upper-tier neighborhood but the zip code meant that he was apparently doing fairly well for himself.

The small porch was clean and adorned with a porch swing. A little ashtray sat underneath the swing, indicating that Charlie was a smoker but opted not to smoke inside. There was no doorbell, so Jack knocked on the door, realizing as he stepped back that he could hear the murmuring of a television from inside.

After several seconds, the door was answered by a middle-aged woman. Her hair had been dyed partially black at some point in the recent past, but her natural blonde strands stood out. She was wearing an athletic tank top and a ratty-looking pair of sweatpants. She was also wearing a lot of makeup, especially the black eyeliner that made her eyes appear a bit too bright.

"Yeah?" she asked. "Who're you?"

For a few seconds, Jack was speechless. He was afraid they'd somehow gotten the wrong house. Unless maybe this was Charlie Foster's wife. But a quick glance at her left hand showed no sign of a wedding ring. It did, though, show a tattoo of a vine that wrapped around her wrist.

"We're looking for Charlie Foster. Is this the right house?"

"Depends on who's asking."

Jack had been an agent long enough to know that this response was essentially a *yes*, an answer that typically came from people who were themselves guilty in some fashion or another.

When he moved his arm to retrieve his ID from his jacket pocket, the woman at the door instinctively took a step back. This was a woman that was flinchy and probably well acquainted with trouble in some form or another. Her left hand went back to the door, as if to close it if need be.

"We're Agents Rivers and Gift with the FBI. We just need to speak with Charlie Foster about some developments in a case we're looking into that could concern an organization his mother is tied to."

He made it through the entire statement unhindered, but noticed her eyes darting to the left and her neck going stiff at the sight of his badge. It appeared as if she wanted to peer back into the house. Maybe to warn someone or to make sure someone else in the house was hearing what she was hearing. It told Jack everything he needed to know. Yes, Charlie Foster was home and no, he was not going to take a visit from the FBI lightly.

"Well, he's not home," the woman said.

"Oh, I see," Jack said. "Well, how about you? Could we maybe talk to—"

He heard movement elsewhere within the house. Something that sounded like the shuffling of feet and then the sound of a door opening slowly and very intentionally. His brain was locked into work mode, thinking only of the case, and that was why he made the following comment without even thinking twice about it.

"Back door," he said. In saying it, he was not thinking that Rachel shouldn't even be with him right now, and he didn't think about the fact that there was a tumor growing in her brain and slowly killing her. He didn't think of any of that until Rachel responded as if nothing was different. She practically leapt down the porch stairs and instantly started running for the side of the house. He nearly called out for her but even if he'd decided to do so, the words would have been cut off. Because at the same time, the woman turned and ran into the house, yelling as she went.

"It's the FBI! Move your ass!"

His first instinct was to chase the woman. But then again, the woman was not their point of interest. And if she was running into the house after he'd already heard a door slowly opening as if in secret, he knew that this was going to all end up playing out in the back yard or during a sudden foot chase.

Jack followed after Rachel, sprinting into the front yard and making his way around the side of the house. His eyes were already on the back yard, a little strip of green that connected with a row of sickly hedges along the side. But then, within just a few more steps, he saw a body on the ground.

It was Rachel.

She was on her hands and knees, pushing herself back up. Apparently, she'd fallen while giving chase. Jack had only ever known her to fall or give out on two separate occasions—and both of those had come after she'd discovered the tumor.

"Christ, Rachel," he said. He was more irritated with himself than he was concerned for her. He stopped to help her up but she swatted him away.

"No. Go after him. He's out back. I saw him cutting across the yard."

"Are you su—"

"*Go*, dammit!"

Angry now, Jack continued on toward the back yard. As he got there, he looked to the back of the house. The porch was small and rather rickety, but he could see the woman he'd spoken with standing at the back door, looking out through a window. She was on the phone with someone, speaking very animatedly.

On the far end of the yard, there was a man running into the neighbor's back yard. He had to jump over a small flowerbed that separated the two yards. When the man landed, he stumbled a bit but kept his balance. He then cut around behind the neighbor's garage, making a direct path back to the street.

Moron, Jack thought. The instinct, he supposed, was sound. He was probably cutting back over to the street to get into a car and then speed away. But Jack had no intentions of letting things get that far. Instead of leaping over the flower bed and taking the same route as the assailant, he cut hard to the left, dashing back up toward Charlie Foster's front yard. He pushed himself hard, unsure of which direction the man—presumably Charlie Foster—had gone.

Jack came to the front yard, his eyes already scanning the neighbor's yard and the sidewalk along the street in front of it. Sure enough, Charlie Foster was heading for an old, blue Mazda. When he saw Jack already coming his way having cut him off, Charlie stopped dead in his tracks and tried to quickly change directions. In doing so, his left foot slid slightly in the grass and he almost fell again. It was more than enough of a stumble to allow Jack to catch up with him. Charlie made it no more than three additional steps before Jack reached out, grabbed his shoulder, and threw him to the ground.

Charlie hit pretty hard, nearly bouncing as he rolled over. He attempted to get to his feet, but Jack was there in an instant. He fell on top of Charlie, doing everything he could to pin him down rather than engage in a fight. Charlie tried to wriggle out from underneath him and Jack did end up throwing one attack out. It was a simple knee to the ribs, nothing hard enough to do any real damage, but just enough to make him stop squirming long enough for Jack to pull the man's arms behind his back. He cuffed him quickly and then got to his feet. He looked around, glad that no one had seen the exchange, though he thought he saw movement along the front window of Charlie's house.

"Come on up," Jack said, reaching down and helping Charlie to his feet.

"What the hell do you want me for anyway?" Charlie asked in a slurred, southern accent.

"Well, first, we just wanted to ask you some questions about your little outburst with Life Fulfilled. But given that you and I just had a little footrace, I think there's a whole other conversation we need to have now."

As he pushed Charlie along toward his bureau sedan, he spotted Rachel coming around the side of the house. She looked embarrassed but seemed to be walking perfectly fine. *Maybe,* Jack thought, *she legitimately just slipped.*

But he knew that wasn't the case. Rachel would probably try to deny it, but he knew the truth.

"Good work," Rachel said. "You good?"

"I'm fine," he said as he opened the back door to the sedan and forced Charlie inside. The man still had some fight in him but seemed mostly resigned to how things had worked out. "The question is: how are you?"

"I'm good. Really."

"I've heard that a lot from you lately," he said. "And it's mostly been lies."

"No it hasn't. And you know, I'd really rather not have that conversation right now."

"Fine. Why don't you stay here and make sure Mr. Foster doesn't try making a run for it. I'm going to head inside and have a talk with his lady friend to see what the hell is going on."

"Sounds good."

Jack moved toward the house to do just that and realized that this was the first time in the course of their five-year partnership that he was actually mad at Rachel. It felt odd and he resented her for making him feel such a way, but he also had to once again remind himself that he had gone to her this afternoon. She had not called him up and begged to be part of the case. No, he had gone to her. And now this was what he had to deal with.

As he walked up to the porch again, he looked back to the car. Rachel was standing her ground, not yet inside the car but keeping her eyes on Charlie Foster from the outside. And as he watched her standing in the gathering dusk, Jack couldn't help but wonder what other secrets she might be keeping rom him and just how bad her condition truly was.

CHAPTER THIRTEEN

Rachel noticed the way Jack was walking as he walked out of the house. There was a march to it, as if he had some undefined purpose he was trying to find. She could tell he was angry and assumed it was because of her. But they couldn't let their personal issues get in the way of the case.

"She's clean?" Rachel asked, noting the woman inside the house was not with him.

"She was no help, but we've got nothing to bust her on," Jack said. "She says her name is Rosalie Deetz and she's been dating Charlie for about six months."

"Any clue as to why he'd be running?"

"Nothing I could see. If there's anything at all in the house, I'm sure a thorough look-over will turn something up." He crossed his arms as he stood with her outside of the car while Charlie Foster waited in the back seat. "So what do we do now, Rachel? You can't very well come with me into the office to question him. If anyone who knows about your leave of absence sees you, Anderson is going to find out."

She knew he was right but still felt a bit of resentment at the way he was addressing her. "You're right," she said flatly. "So just take me back to my house. It's not too far out of the way."

"And you're okay with that?"

"No. I hate it. But as much as I hate to admit it, it's the smart move." She smiled out of habit, trying to lighten the mood. "Maybe you just drive slowly and we can question him in the car."

He made the same lazy smile but then cocked his head and changed his expression. "Maybe that's not so crazy," he said. He'd lowered his voice, as if making sure Charlie couldn't hear him. "Get in. Follow my lead."

Rachel was not usually so easygoing when it came to following along with a plan that she didn't know the details to. But the look of curiosity and determination she saw on Jack's face made it a little easier to go along with whatever he had planned.

They both got into the car and as soon as the doors were closed, Jack looked into the back seat, directly at Charlie. "Charlie Foster, yes?"

"Yes," Charlie said. Rachel could tell that he was uneasy but was doing his very best to keep a brave face on.

"Any reason you ran like your house was on fire when you heard the FBI was at the door?"

Charlie looked back and forth between them, trying his best to size them up. Having interrogated several hundred people during her time as an agent, Rachel knew that this was the moment where the criminal tried to make a decision. Did they deny any wrong-doing or did they admit just enough to warrant a slap on the wrist with the hope that the feds would go away happy with a small victory while there was a much larger crime lurking elsewhere?

Ten seconds passed and Charlie said nothing. He looked back toward the house, where Rosalie Deetz was still watching, now from a small crack in the front door.

Jack took his eyes away from Charlie and looked at Rachel. He sighed, shook his head, and said, "Damn, Gift. What do you want to do here? Is it even worth the trouble? The day's over and I just want to get home."

"Hey, a bust is a bust," Rachel said. "What did the girlfriend say?"

"Not a thing." Again, looking back to Charlie, he said: "Come on, just tell us. Why'd you run. No, wait…a better question: why do you think we were here in the first place?"

"Hell if I know," Charlie said. Rachel saw that he was clearly confused over the way this conversation was taking place.

"I really think you're lying to me," Jack said. "But look, I'm going to level with you. We know you did it. We have enough evidence and if you keep denying it, we're going to have to make a whole big thing out of this. But if you just tell us right now…come clean and tell us—*just* the two of us—then we can make a neat little bust. You'll get a slap on the wrist, maybe a few fines, but you won't go to jail. Do you follow me?"

"You expect me to believe a word you say?"

"Hey, I don't care one way or the other. Either way this goes down, we're getting a bust. I'm a happy guy either way. You're the one who gets to decide if this is going to be a long and drawn-out process or if it's over for everyone—including *you*—in just a matter of hours."

Rachel could tell by the way Charlie's eyes were looking all around that he was about to reveal something. But at the same time, she also noticed that he looked merely nervous. Whatever he was about to admit to might be criminal at its core, but it wasn't going to be involvement of murder or malice.

"There's some taped to the back of the toilet," Charlie said. "And then there's some more on the underside of the drawer on the table on my bedside."

Drugs, then, Rachel thought. *And certainly something more than pot or pills if he's hiding it like this and takes off running at the mention of the FBI at his door.* As far as Rachel was concerned, this meant he was very likely not their killer. Before she could allow the defeat of the moment to settle in over her, she jumped right back into their little performance.

"And that's it?" she said.

"Yes, I swear."

Jack looked back at the house, solely coming out of character. "You made a good choice, Mr. Foster."

"Man…I had to. I didn't have a choice."

"What do you mean?" Rachel asked.

Charlie shook his head and looked through the window, out into the street. "My mom is sick, man. Cancer. She's…she's probably not going to beat it. The chemo helps, but…and the bills are just too damn ridiculous. I had to do *something*."

She could see Jack reaching for the door handle, likely intending to go inside to see what sort of drugs Charlie Foster was hiding. He looked a bit more upset about the way this had all played out than Rachel had expected.

"Mr. Foster, just as a second-hand matter, can you tell us what you were doing yesterday afternoon between the hours of four and six?"

At first, he seemed perplexed by the question but then put some thought into it. "I worked until five thirty yesterday. I left work and headed to Bull's Bar—this bar me and Rosalie go to."

"Where do you work?

"Townsend's Auto Glass and Repair."

"So there would be at least one or two people to confirm that you were indeed there yesterday afternoon?"

"Yeah. At least five."

"And how far away from work is the bar?"

"Maybe five minutes. It's why we go there…because it's so close to my work."

"Was it busy when you got there?" Rachel asked.

"Not really. Maybe a dozen or so people. But what does any of that have to do with anything?"

"Maybe nothing," Rachel said. "Just checking on something."

With a heavy sigh, Jack finally opened up his door. "Well, I'm going to head inside for bit to look those places over. I'll be right back."

He closed the door a bit harder than was necessary and when he made his way back to the house, Rachel saw the rigid way he walked. He was irritated and upset, likely for a number of different reasons. She couldn't help but feel bad, but at the same time, he'd brought some of it on himself.

And speaking of feeling bad for people, she glanced back at Charlie Foster. He was also watching Jack walk back to his house and, like Jack, there was a defeated posture to him. Rachel's heart actually went out to the man; he'd been pushed to dealing drugs to help pay for his mother's medical bills. She supposed maybe his financial situation was why he'd had such a severe reaction when Life Fulfilled had informed him about the waiting list.

She sat with Charlie Foster in silence, both of them now looking to the house as Jack stepped inside to investigate a crime they'd accidentally stumbled into—all while their killer was still free.

***

With a much more agreeable Charlie Foster in the back of the bureau sedan, Jack drove Rachel home. When they exchanged a tense and brief goodbye, Charlie didn't even seem to notice, and Rachel assumed he was far too bogged down in his own thoughts, probably starting to worry about his immediate future.

Rachel walked through her front door just after 7:30. Grandma Tate and Paige were talking together in the kitchen. Rachel joined them, finding them huddled around a bowl of popcorn. She saw two plates in the sink, smeared with red from a simple spaghetti dinner.

"Mommy!" Paige said, upon seeing her. She rushed over and gave her mother a hug, munching popcorn the entire time.

"Hey, Paige. I'm so sorry I wasn't here this evening."

"That's okay. I went over to Suzanne's house. We played Animal Crossing and then went outside and jumped rope. And then Grandma made spaghetti and then popcorn!"

"I see. Sounds like you had a pretty great afternoon."

Paige nodded as she returned back to the bowl of popcorn. Rachel joined them at the table and the following fifteen minutes were spent with Paige recounting her day. They also took turns trying to toss popcorn in each other's mouths. Paige seemed very happy, probably as happy as she'd been ever since her father had walked away. And as this understanding settled on her, Rachel realized that she hadn't spoken to him in three weeks. They'd have to speak about how to carry on to start divorce proceedings soon enough and she wondered how to go about it while keeping Paige out of all of the drama.

As 8 o'clock came around, Paige headed upstairs to brush her teeth and get ready for bed. With the sound of her footfalls over their heads on the second floor, Rachel and Grandma Tate tidied up for dinner. As she set the now-empty popcorn bowl in the sink, Rachel looked over to Grandma Tate, quite certain that things had seemed at least slightly off with her ever since she'd returned home.

"I really do appreciate you helping me out this afternoon."

Grandma Tate shrugged it off, as if it were really no big deal at all. "One of the reasons I came to stay with you was so I could help you out." She paused and leaned against the kitchen counter, a frown on her face. "Of course, I had no idea that you intended to keep working. Now, I'm inclined to say it's none of my business, but seeing as how Paige is my great-granddaughter, I suppose it is *partly* my business. Your time is short and though she may not be acutely aware of it, she *will* come to understand it one day. She'll come to understand than in your final days, you continued to choose work over her."

"But that's not what I'm doing." She was close to tears, maybe because the comments were a little closer to the truth than she cared to admit.

"Are you sure about that, Rachel?" She paused for a moment, as if wondering if she'd gone too far with the comment. But she carried on, maybe thinking that now that the line had been crossed, she may as well forge on. "I don't fault you for it. You've always been career-oriented, and I have no doubt it's because of what you do—stopping bad people from doing bad things. I can't imagine the sort of drive that puts into someone."

Grandma Tate surprised Rachel when she stepped forward and wrapped her in a small, fragile hug. "I'm here for you, doll. I always have been and always will be. Watching after Paige these past few weeks has been some of the happiest days of this latter part of my life. But as for me and you—I'm just worried about you, Rachel. I don't want your final moments to be out on a case where that thing in your brain decides it's had enough. If you're truly coming to the end of your life, I do believe it needs to be with your daughter."

Rachel said nothing because she didn't need to say anything. Everything Grandma Tate was saying were things Rachel had thought. She just wished it weren't so damned hard to step away from her job.

"Now," Grandma Tate said. "I've said what I have to say. But you're a grown woman, Rachel. You make your own decisions."

Rachel wiped a few tears away, nodding. "I know. This case Jack is working on now, the victims are—"

"Nope," Grandma Tate said, interrupting her. "I don't need to hear about it, nor do I want to. But you do what you think is best for you. Just…well, please don't forget that there's a precious little girl back here. She's doing fine, but she's going to look back on this time and be very confused if you don't sort things out soon."

That said, Grandma Tate gave a quick little nod and excused herself from the kitchen. Rachel sat down at the table by herself and let the words sink in. Nothing Grandma Tate had said was anything new, but hearing them spoken in such a loving way seemed to make it all *feel* new.

Moments later, when she heard Paige's footfalls coming back down the stairs, she walked into the living room. Paige was dressed in her pajamas and though she was clearly tired, she was smiling and doing her best to milk every extra minute she could.

After saying goodnight to Grandma Tate, Paige took Rachel by the hand and led her upstairs. As Rachel tucked her in, Paige looked up at her with curious eyes. "Grandma Tate said you went somewhere with Jack…Jack from work. Is that right?"

"Yes."

"So are you still working?" There was no accusatory tone in her little voice; she was legitimately curious.

"Not like I used to. Jack just needed some help on this one case he's working on."

"I bet he'd miss you if you stopped all the time."

"Yeah, I think he would, too." She hugged Paige close and snuggled into the curve of her little neck and shoulders.

"So don't make him lonely," Paige said.

"Jack will be okay. Besides…don't you want me here?"

"I mean…sure, yeah. But can't you still help him when I'm in school? You like your job, don't you?"

"I do."

"So then do it," she said, giggling. "Don't be silly. But you and Grandma Tate *could* just stay here all day if you want."

"Yeah, and what would we do?"

"I dunno. Play games…drink tea."

They giggled together at this and Rachel ended up not being able to leave her daughter's side. After a while, Paige fell asleep, her little snores like the purring of a cat. Rachel kissed her daughter's forehead and even then still could not bring herself to leave her side.

So she lay there for a moment, not at all surprised that Paige's words were carrying more weight than those from Grandma Tate.

"But can't you still help him when I'm in school? You like your job, don't you?"

Rachel lay there for a long time in the gloom of Paige's room. She thought of Jack and of the two victims they'd come across—of how their already shortened lives had become drastically shorter. They'd been robbed of moments like these, with children and other loved ones, moments where they could process and find peace.

And, job or not, what sort of human being would she be if she turned a blind eye to that?

CHAPTER FOURTEEN

It was a nice change of pace not to sit in the parking lot of a medical facility to wait for his next victim. Even being in the immediate vicinity of hospitals or medical specialists made him feel ill. For some reason, he'd always viewed such places as even worse than cemeteries. The reek of death and sickness just seemed to emanate from them.

Now, though, he was sitting in a place that was the exact opposite of a hospital. He was parked behind a club, not a large one but not just some small, hole-in-the-wall dive, either. It was the type of place that would have a bar stretched out across the back wall, and a large stage for live music on the other end. With his windows rolled down a bit, he could hear a grinding bass line and a slightly off-time drumbeat. The band, according to the club's website, was called Ruckus and they played a variety of '90s alternative music.

His next target was inside. He knew this because the idiot had posted it on Facebook. He was looking at the post on his phone right now, the smiling moron standing right in front of the club with RUCKUS on the marquee behind him. His post simply read #bucketlist.

"Bucket list," he muttered ironically.

He understood the appeal of bucket lists but also thought such a popular term should serve as a wakeup call to humanity. If people would just live their lives to the fullest from the start, there would be no need to push exciting events or desires back further and further until you realize your days are indeed numbered. Anyone keeping a bucket list and touting it as this noble thing to keep up with was, in his opinion, wasting their life.

Like his next victim. Twenty-nine years old and diagnosed with a mild liver disease. It was mild, but there was also no cure for it. From what he gathered, the man would have another two years to live…maybe two and a half, depending on how he responded to the experimental medicines that were supposed to help slow the progression of the disease.

This man, Troy Hetfield, was at the very bottom of the Life Fulfilled list. He'd just gotten on the waiting list five days ago qhich would usually not make him an instant target. But when a new waiting-list member was so ignorantly posting every detail of his very short life on social media, making it easy to track him down, what was the sense in waiting?

He had no idea how long the concert would last, so he'd been parked behind the place, three cars over from Hetfield's for the past hour and a half. Ruckus was apparently a decently popular band; he estimated that there had to be at least a thousand people or so inside, which was probably flirting with the maximum occupancy numbers for a place of this size.

The current song came to an end and he heard a muffled roar of applause as the opening riff to the next song kicked in. He actually knew it, sort of. Some song by Nirvana. The crowd went nuts. He hoped it was a sign that the band was nearing the end of their show.

He sat and waited. He checked Hetfield's Facebook feed again and saw that he'd posted pictures of himself with a girl he'd apparently run into at the show. He was near the front of the stage, tucked in tightly among other sweaty concertgoers.

He then looked to his list, which had been growing over the past several weeks. He had it all typed into the notes app on his phone, an exact copy of the physical copy sitting on his desk at home. He had been checking names off as he eliminated them. It was then, as he looked over the shortening list, that the Nirvana song ended. The crowd cheered and within about three minutes, he noticed people starting to come walking around the side of the club. Many of them were heading to the parking lot across the street, and into the adjoining parking garage. But Hetfield would not be headed that way. No, according to the Facebook post, he'd been granted backstage access. Even though he was not yet officially under the umbrella of Life Fulfilled, he was still getting favors here and there due to his recent bad news.

So even with the concert over, he figured he had a while longer to wait. The again, with a liver disease, he doubted Hetfield would do any drinking—so what else was there to do backstage at a rock concert?

He sat in his car as midnight came and went, watching traffic trickling out of the parking garage and lot across the street to his right. He wondered how many people behind the wheels of those vehicles had close loved ones who were terminally ill or on the cusp of receiving that sort of news. He knew it was morbid, but he thought about the speed and suddenness with which life could go from happy and thriving to on the brink of death. Often it was as simple as a single doctor's visit—and he found that both fascinating and horrifying.

As he considered all of this, he watched as one of the back doors to the club opened up. A man came out—a man who was not Troy Hetfield. The man looked around the parking lot, stepped beside a dumpster, and unbuttoned his pants He urinated quickly and then stepped back inside.

Not too long after that, maybe three or four minutes by his estimation, the door opened again. This time, Troy Hetfield *did* step out. He was accompanied by the young lady that he'd taken the latest Facebook picture with. They walked together to his car and stood outside of it for a moment. As he watched, Troy and this woman spoke and then kissed for a bit, only to speak once more and then focus more on the kissing part of things.

It was getting so hot and heavy that for a moment, he wondered if they were going to end up having sex right there against the car. But in the end, the woman broke away with a huge smile. He used this moment as a distraction, quietly opening his door and stepping out into the night. He crouched and remained low, hiding between his car and the one parked next to him. Hetfield's was just two cars beyond this, allowing him to hear the end of the conversation the couple was having.

"…and next weekend," the woman was saying.

"Yeah, I think that should still work. But, you know, you can come with me now. To my place."

"I want to, but…you know that's not a good idea."

"Sounds like a *great* idea to me."

The woman giggled again, but was not giving in. "Patience, Troy."

"I know, I know."

The woman's shadow passed by his car as she made her way back over to the parking garage. When she was far enough out of sight, he feared that he'd missed his window of opportunity. He was going to have be a little risky, he supposed.

He stood up and saw that Hetfield was watching the woman go. He'd not yet even made a move to get back into his car. Hetfield appeared to be deeply in love or very horny—or maybe a touch of both.

Hetfield slowly turned his head, having seen the flicker of motion as he'd gotten to his feet.

"Troy, what's up?" he said.

Hetfield smiled for a moment, tilting his head. "Hey. Do I…do I know you?"

"Nah, not well." He walked around the front of the first of the two cars that were separating them, keeping his left hand low and just slightly behind him. He offered his right hand, though, as if wanting a shake. "I don't know if you remember or not. We met at that other show not too long ago. But I don't remember the name."

He had advanced to within hand-shaking distance and Troy, still smiling slightly and clearly confused, started to shake his head. "What show would that b—"

He brought his left hand up, bringing the leather sap up with expert speed and precision. The sound it made against Hetfield's head was a hollow *thunk* that was not terribly unlike the muted bass drum coming through the club's walls. Not being a leftie, he knew he didn't get his full strength behind it, so as Hetfield tottered and reeled back, almost falling over, he swapped it over to his right hand.

The second attack was much stronger. It caught Hetfield right in the center of his forehead, right between the eyes. There was a crunching noise as the bridge of his nose was pulverized. With that, Hetfield's knees gave out and he went to the ground right away.

Standing there and looking down at Hetfield, he regretted that he had to move away so quickly. God only knew who else might come out of that backstage door and even now, there were cars coming out of the parking garage, their headlights coming dangerously close to skirting over the scene of the crime.

He left Troy Hetfield on the ground, walking back over to his car. He stuffed the leather sap beneath his driver's seat, started the engine, and pulled out onto the street. He'd sat and waited for nearly two hours and the act itself had taken less than five seconds. Still, it was worth it. And he could hardly wait until he got to the next red light so he could wipe yet another name off of the Life Fulfilled waiting list.

CHAPTER FIFTEEN

Rachel walked behind the coroner, a man she'd never seen before, although he still felt familiar. He was very tall and incredibly thin, almost like a skeleton that had simply had human skin draped over it and called a human. He was leading her down a long hallway that looked to be made of steel and was adorned with countless doors. Each door looked the same, made of either steel or some sort of silicon.

"She's been waiting for you," the coroner said over his shoulder.

"I know," Rachel said. "I'm so sorry I'm late."

The floor began to glow slightly as they continued to walk. It looked almost like something out of a spaceship from a science fiction movie, all white and blue lights along metal surfaces. Finally, they came to the door they were searching for. When the coroner held the door open for her, he smiled at her, revealing a mouthful of back teeth. "Step inside," he said in a voice that sounded like a hurricane passing through a cavern.

Inside, he stepped in front of her. They were greeted with a room that seemed to have no end, metal containment drawers installed in a wall that stretched on forever. Fortunately, they did not have to walk a length the equal of the corridor they had used to get here. No, the drawer in question was right in front of them.

As the coroner led her to it, the temperature of the room dropped substantially. Rachel could see her breath in front of her, a little cloud that hovered for far too long and then dissipated.

"Feel free to do the honors," the coroner said in that same horrid voice.

Rachel stepped forward and grabbed the handle to the locker. It clicked open easily and when she pulled it out, it rolled along on tracks that sounded far too much like the snapping of knuckles.

The body on the slab was covered in a sheet that was speckled with little droplets of blood here and there. She reached out and grabbed the sheet, slowly pulling it back to reveal the face.

Rachel gasped and took a step back. She was looking down at herself. Her skin was pale, her eyes were closed, and there was dried blood matted in her hair.

"How?" Rachel asked. "Why…?"

But the coroner had no answer for her. On the slab, the dead Rachel opened her eyes and grinned.

Rachel screamed.

The scream tore her out of the nightmare with such ferocity that she almost fell right out of bed. And as she did her best to get control of her senses, she realized that it may have been more than the nightmare that had stirred her awake. It sounded like her phone was ringing, too.

As she slapped around on the bedside table for it, her heart slammed madly in her chest. The digital numbers on her clock read 4:31. The call had to be from Jack. Jack and Director Anderson were the only ones who ever called her at such an hour. The absurdness of the moment, interlaced with the surreal dream, made her wonder if she'd really put in that two weeks' notice after all. Had *that* been a dream? Why else would Jack be calling her at such an hour? She grabbed the phone and brought it to her ear. "Yeah?"

Sure enough, it *was* Jack on the other end. "Hey, Rachel. I should, uh…I should let you know that I instantly regret calling you. Forget I called, okay?"

"What? Jack, wait…"

There was silence on the other end, and she was certain she'd somehow missed the click of him hanging up. But after a few moments, his voice was there again, soft and in her ear.

"There's been another murder. Not sure if it's our guy, but it was a knock on the head. From the little we know about him, he was recently diagnosed with a deadly and rare liver disease. I thought you'd want to know and then by the time I realized you weren't my partner anymore, your phone had started ringing. I blame it on being woken up just after four by the phone."

"It's okay, Jack. I appreciate it. Will you come get me?"

"No."

"Then send me the address and I'll come on my own."

"No, Rachel, I can't keep let—"

"Then what the hell did you call me for, Jack?"

"Habit."

The line went quiet again and she eventually heard one of Jack's patented long, exhaustive sighs. "Damn. Fine. I'll be there in twenty minutes."

She opened her mouth to thank him, but this time the call *had* come to an end. Rachel, surprised to find that she wasn't tired at all, slowly slid out of bed and thought of how to best communicate what was going on to Grandma Tate. She left her bedroom and walked down the hall to the guest room. Rachel raised her hand on Grandma Tate's door, realizing before she even knocked that she was starting to cry.

***

The body was still on the pavement when they arrived. It was a male, twenty-nine years old, by the name of Troy Hetfield. His face was in much worse shape than the small bit of blood on it suggested. The bridge of his nose had been broken and it almost looked as if that portion of his head had tried to collapse in on itself.

A deputy with the police was on the scene with about eight others. Forensics had already arrived, kneeling by the body and doing their work under the glow of headlights and a few portable halogen lamps. The deputy stood with Rachel and Jack while forensics did their work. He looked to be a bit older than fifty, with the beginnings of a beer gut and a deeply receding hairline.

"The body was discovered by another concertgoer," the deputy said. "We think the body was found very soon after the attack because the witness said the blood was still coming from the wound in above the nose."

"And this person saw no one else out here?" Jack asked.

"No," the deputy said. "But they did say there were still cars coming out of the parking garage over there. There was a concert here tonight, a pretty big local cover band. We were able to confirm with the band that the deceased had special backstage passes. Some sort of special privilege because of some bad news the guy had been dealt recently."

"Is that how it was discovered the victim had been diagnosed with liver disease?" Rachel asked.

"Yeah, as far as I can tell."

Now that they had a name, Rachel pulled her phone out and navigated to the Life Fulfilled waiting list. As she suspected, Troy Hetfield was indeed listed there. The odd thing, though, was that he was the very last name on the list. Based on the scant information provided by the list, he'd only been added a few days ago.

"There are security measures in place at the doors, correct?" Jack asked.

"Yeah," the deputy said. "And we've already spoken to the head of security. He allowed us to have a look at the night's logs. Nine hundred and eleven people attended the show tonight and only four were turned away out of refusal to pass through metal detectors at the door."

73

"What about backstage?" Rachel asked.

"Doesn't matter," the deputy replied. "Even those with backstage passes have to be admitted through the front gates."

"Any security footage?" Rachel asked.

"Not from back here. There are eight different camera *in* the club and two right there up front at the gates. But there are none back here. I'm told it's something of a controversial measure so that the bands aren't easily ensnared in illegal activities like drugs and things like that. Seems ass backwards to me, but…"

He shrugged, as if that was the end of the conversation as far as he was concerned.

Rachel stepped closer to the body. Of the two forensics officers, only one was still kneeling down by the body. The other was standing and typing something into a smart pad.

"Anything of note?" Rachel asked.

"He was attacked from the front for sure," the kneeling man said. "I can see at least two different attacks, one right there, above the left brow, and the other, stronger one, right between the eyes. In terms of any physical evidence for you, I'm afraid there's nothing."

Rachel nodded, taking another look at the body. A young man, just a few years younger than her, already dealing with terrible news…and here he was, dead, because someone else had decided to take whatever time he had left away from him. She was sad about having left Paige again, and the conversation she'd had with Grandma Tate before she'd left the house had been tense, but looking down at Troy Hetfield assured her that she'd made the right choice. She was going to catch this bastard if it was the last thing she did.

She and Jack stepped slightly away from the forensics team and the deputy. A chill crept its way through Rachel as she tried to keep a lid on her anger.

"I think it's now safe to say that with this Life Fulfilled waitlist, we also have the kill-list," she said.

"Agreed," Jack said. "But there's no order to follow. I mean, Jesus, this guy was just added a few days ago. How did the killer know?"

"Seems like something we need to find out," Rachel said. "We have a list of people he may be looking for, but no MO yet. No evidence, no leads."

"We need to speak to this guy's family," Jack said. "I know it's going to be tough because they just found out, but—"

"Let's go, then," she said. "If they've also been struggling with the news of his diagnosis, I think you'll find that the strength and resolve of these people is going to be more than you're expecting."

He gave her a strange look; she couldn't decide if it was one of irritation or resolve. In the final few hours of dark, she decided she didn't care. She just wanted to get to the family and figure out what sort of person might have wanted to kill Troy Hetfield. She knew far too well how precious time was and she did not intend to waste a single second.

CHAPTER SIXTEEN

When they arrived at the Hetfield residence, they found a typical pair of parents who had just been given the devastating news of a child being murdered. Sadly, it was something Rachel was far too familiar with. The mother was in an almost catatonic state. She sat at the kitchen table, partially collapsed onto it. Every now and then she would let out a guttural wail and then resume her silence.

As for the father, he had elected to do what he could to be the strong one. Rachel could clearly see that he was struggling to contain his own emotions. She could see it in his eyes and the way he moved rigidly around the kitchen. He was drinking a cup of tea and every time he set the mug down on the counter, Rachel thought it was going to shatter from the force of it.

"Mr. Hetfield, I know it's hard to think past anything other than the news you received in the last few hours," Rachel said. "But anything you can tell us now will give us a much better shot at who might be doing this."

"Troy isn't the only one," Jack added. "Over the course of the last four days, two other people with terminal illnesses have been killed. And they've all been on the waiting list for Life Fulfilled."

"My God," Mr. Hetfield said. And with just those two words, Rachel saw even more of that emotion trying to stay locked up inside. His lips were trembling and the hand not holding the tea mug clenched and unclenched habitually. "But Troy…he was just placed on the list."

"Yes, we know," Jack said. "And I think that might be what we need from you. It's been so recent for you, we were wondering if you might be able to walk us through what the process for signing up looks like. We have to assume that the killer somehow has access to the waiting list. So everything we can know about it from the patient side of things may help us immensely."

"Oh, sure…um…" He trailed off, looking to his wife. "She did most of it, but I was there, you know. She—"

His wife let out another of her heartbroken wails and this time sat up in her chair. She left streaks of tears on the table and her face was red and swollen from crying.

"Sorry about that," Mr. Hetfield said, but he did not move. It was clear that he did not want to let his wife out of his sight, wanting to keep a check on her. "The first step, of course, was just getting in touch with them. We called the office and they sent us a questionnaire. It wasn't very long…maybe three pages…"

"Six," Mrs. Hetfield said, her voice raw and raspy. "Six pages. And then we also needed copies of Troy's most recent medical records. That was the hardest…hardest part."

She started to weep again and Rachel wasn't sure exactly how much help she was going to be—which was completely understandable.

"Was the questionnaire fairly standard?" Rachel asked. "No questions or items that seemed out of place?"

"None that I can recall," Mr. Hetfield said. His wife only shook her head. "But I can let you see the questionnaire if you want."

"If you could forward it to us when we're done here, that may be helpful," Rachel said.

"Anyway, after that, we sent it all in and they called us back within a few days. Certainly no more than a week. They told us from the start that there was a waiting list, so that wasn't a surprise."

"Do you have any idea how many people were ahead of you?" Jack asked.

"I think it was twenty-one or twenty-two people. Something like that. They said it could be up to six months, maybe longer. But we knew—or well, we *thought*—Troy had more time." He stopped and let out his first true sign of grief since they'd arrived. He wept openly for a few seconds, wiping the tears away with his hands as if it made him angry to do so. "And if he had more time, we figured that made sense. People with more dire needs should come first."

"The doctor," Mrs. Hetfield said from her post at the table. "He was…he was strange, right?"

"Oh," Mr. Hetfield said. He nodded but also rolled his eyes a bit, like he didn't think it was really worth mentioning. "Yeah, there was a doctor we had to speak to just before Troy was given a spot on the waiting list."

"Your standard family physician?" Rachel asked.

"No, this was a guy that works for Life Fulfilled."

This seemed peculiar to Rachel. She'd seen no form of doctor's office or examination rooms while they'd been in the Life Fulfilled building. It had also not come up in any of their conversations about the organization. Rachel thought it might be one of the more prominent features or talking points about a place like Life Fulfilled.

"Did you have any opinion about this doctor?" Rachel asked.

"Not really. I mean…he's just a doctor, you know? From what I gathered, this guy is a retired doctor that Life Fulfilled has on a retainer. There were no real examinations to speak of at all. He basically just went over Troy's records with us and asked about the history of his current condition. That sort of thing." He fought with emotion for another moment or two but after a few seconds, managed to continue. "No one ever came out and said as much, but I'm pretty sure he's like the last line of defense to make sure no one is trying to con the foundation…that no one is faking their illness."

"And after speaking with him…?" Jack said.

"We were put on the list."

"And do you happen to know his name?"

"Sorry, but I don't remember."

"Lucas," Mrs. Hetfield said, her head once again lowered to the table surface as she drew in large, deep breaths. "Dr. Ben Lucas."

Rachel committed the name to memory, looking over at Jack. She noted the look of slight confusion on Jack's face, his brow slightly bunched up and his eyes thoughtful. She assumed he was thinking the same thing she was: the fact that no one at Life Fulfilled had yet mentioned such a doctor seemed odd. It was almost as if they were trying to hide the position from the prying eyes of people outside of the foundation.

More than that, it gave them a potential lead and a reason to quickly get out of the Hetfields' house, allowing them the proper time and environment in which to grieve.

CHAPTER SEVENTEEN

Because Rachel wasn't supposed to be on the case, they couldn't just drive to the office and use the database to look for information on Dr. Ben Lucas. It was the first time Rachel truly felt like a hindrance on the case, wondering if maybe she was indeed making a mistake by insisting that she be there—not that Jack's instincts of including her were helping at all. To make up for this, they decided to take things "old school," as Jack put it.

He headed for the nearest library while calling up Monty in the records department again. Per usual, he kept the call on speaker mode so Rachel could be kept in the loop. Monty answered on the third ring and, like last time, seemed anxious to assist.

"Monty, I need you to get me some information on a doctor by the name of Ben Lucas. Anything we have. Criminal records, personal information, whatever we can get."

"I can do that. Is this a top priority sort of thing?"

"I wouldn't be bothering you with this if it wasn't a top priority sort of thing. And listen…send me PDFs of whatever you find. I'd like to have copies of this on hand."

"I can do that. Give me about fifteen minutes, would you?"

"That's perfect," Jack said, ending the call.

"You know," Rachel said, "I don't quite understand the need for a retired doctor on staff at a place like Life Fulfilled. I totally understand the need for a final line of defense, but wouldn't a foundation like that just be willing to take the word of non-retired doctors? It just seems weird to me."

"I thought so, too," Jack said. "But I also know how very tight this country can be when it comes to anything medical or related to healthcare. I can fully understand a foundation like theirs wanting to make sure they have every base covered several times over."

Rachel mulled this over as they reached the library. She understood Jack's point, but at the same time, she started to think that having that last say in whether or not someone was worthy of those kinds of benefits was a heavy responsibility.

When Jack pulled the car into the library parking lot, he checked his email on his phone. "Monty just delivered those documents," he said

"Honestly, I was expecting a message saying he couldn't find anything."

"And if there are records on a doctor, there's bound to be a story there," Rachel said.

"So let's get inside and put it together."

They walked into the library, a two-story building that was quiet, given the time of day (10:40 in the morning) on a weekday. They settled into a small table in a corner on the first floor and started looking over the PDFs Monty had sent them. There really wasn't much of a story at all, but enough to warrant a criminal file. Before becoming a doctor, Benjamin Lucas had been arrested twice in his twenties, while in med school, for taking part in protests that got out of hand. One of the protests had been in front of a laboratory that had been working on what would later be known as stem-cell research. It had turned violent, and Lucas had ended up tackling a cop to the ground. He'd been fined and spent three weeks in prison. There was also a file on Lucas in terms of his name coming up in past cases where medical issues or discrepancies had popped up in active police cases. He'd never been brought in for questioning or as a suspect, but his name had been flagged on two occasions in the state of Tennessee.

"Tennessee," Rachel said. "Looks like there might be stories about this guy that wouldn't have naturally fallen into a criminal record."

They walked over to the closest available computer, an old Dell desktop model that seemed to populate most public libraries. Rachel took the seat and pulled up Google, typing in *Doctor Benjamin Lucas Tennessee*. There was a list of hits within seconds, but the headlines of the first few links told them what they needed to know.

"Jackpot," Jack said as Rachel opened up the first result.

For the next ten minutes, they read several different articles, all from reputable news outlets, about a surprising bit of history pertaining to Dr. Benjamin Lucas. Eleven years ago, Dr. Lucas had been stripped of his medical license in the state of Tennessee. It was a very basic story, though a sad one. Lucas had been treating a terminal cancer patient from their home and had administered almost three times the necessary dose of morphine. For a doctor with a stellar medical record to that point, a mistake of that caliber was practically unheard of. During the trial that followed, Lucas never denied it and made no excuses. He also showed very little remorse. When people started digging, more situations like that arose. And though there were no other deaths linked to him, there were several instances of the patient's case worsening and needing additional medical treatment.

"Okay, so," Jack said, "I'm going to assume Life Fulfilled knows about all of this. If not, they need to do some serious recalibration on their process for employee background checks. But how is it that the people who are applying for Life fulfilled benefits aren't doing their basic research and learning all of this?"

Rachel stared at the last screen she'd pulled up. She thought she knew the answer to this, and it was pretty depressing. "They might be doing their research. But what they're facing…when they look at the benefits Life Fulfilled offers, they may not give a damn."

"And as for Life Fulfilled…I'm guessing Wes Dalton and all of the bigwigs probably know that. And I can only assume that a disgraced doctor is going to come with a *much* smaller price tag than an actual on-staff physician."

Rachel closed the browser window, conflicted. If they put this in the face of Life Fulfilled and anyone outside of the organization dug even the slightest little bit, it would ruin the foundation. And while Rachel was all about crooked people getting what they deserve, she also knew that Life Fulfilled was indeed fulfilling the wishes of the terminally ill and assisting them in their day-to-day lives.

She forced herself to look beyond that, though. She focused on what they knew about Lucas getting his license suspended. Giving someone three times the amount of necessary morphine was indeed a huge error. And the fact that he'd made no excuses or given any proper explanations seemed odd.

"Do you think he could have killed that patient on purpose?" she asked.

"Don't know. His responses to it during the investigation certainly make me think it might have been a possibility."

"Well," Rachel said, getting to her feet. "If he is indeed working for Life Fulfilled, he's doing so without a medical license. And I think if we hold that over his head, he might be pretty forthcoming with any information he might have."

They started walking out of the library and Rachel realized that she felt great—maybe better than she had since getting her diagnosis. Her head was clear and pain free, she had a good deal of energy, and there was no added pressure. It might be a bit dishonest of her, but to know that this wasn't her case—that she was, in fact, not even technically an agent at the moment—made her feel as if an immense weight had been lifted from her shoulders. And with that sense of clarity, she started to consider the idea that maybe Dr. Lucas was getting a taste of his old life in working through Life Fulfilled. And if he *had* intentionally killed that patient several years ago, at the same time he'd harmed others, maybe he was remembering what it had been like.

Maybe he was remembering that he'd enjoyed it and was starting over again, only this time in a much more immediate way.

CHAPTER EIGHTEEN

Rachel continued to feel almost as if she were being babysat while Jack drove the car to Dr. Lucas's house. It was not all that uncommon for him to be behind the wheel while she kept an eye on directions via GPS, but it felt different this time. It was very clear that she was more or less a backseat driver for this case. But again, she sat in the realization that she felt incredible, so she didn't question it at all.

They'd elected to try Lucas's house before contacting Life Fulfilled, figuring it would be much more beneficial to go directly to the source than to jump over whatever hurdles and obstacles the foundation might set out before them. The first sign that Lucas had fallen from grace came in the location of his home. Call it a stereotype or not, but Rachel had been through enough neighborhoods and communities to know that the vast majority of doctors lived in nicer neighborhoods—neighborhoods where the houses might looked very much alike, but the price tags were in the high six figures or more. A lot of them were also located near hospitals or universities.

But Dr. Benjamin Lucas lived in a rather basic-looking neighborhood. There was nothing at all wrong with it but it simply wasn't the sort of place she'd ever known a doctor to live. They passed by a few modest houses and then turned into a small two-lane thoroughfare that passed through a chain of apartments and townhouses. They found a parking spot just a few spaces away from Lucas's townhouse and stepped out into a quiet corner of a subdivision.

After knocking on the door twice and not getting an answer, it became apparent that he wasn't home. They both walked away from the door, sensing the same issues ahead without having to actually verbalize them. In fact, neither of them spoke it out loud until they were back in the car and Jack was pulling out of the parking spot.

"We're going to have to tip off Life Fulfilled," he said.

"And if he's not there in the office and the foundation *is* up to something," Rachel said, "they'll have every opportunity to tip him off or give us the runaround about patient confidentiality."

Jack waited several seconds before adding: "You know that if it gets to that point you have to sit the rest of it out, right? If we have to go through official channels for paperwork and getting access to a doctor or his records—"

"I know," Rachel said, once again feeling out of place. "And if that happens, I'll shut up and back away."

Jack chuckled and shook his head. "*You'll* shut up?"

Rachel shrugged and smiled at him. "Eh, we'll see."

They rushed back to the Life Fulfilled offices with the possibility of a strong lead growing between them. There was certainly something sinister about the idea of an unlicensed doctor going around and distributing what he thought of as mercy kills, but it also felt like a very far-flung theory. By the time they reached the office, Rachel thought there was a morbid sort of sense to it. After all, working with an organization like Life Fulfilled would give such a killer very easy access to a list of victims. It was almost too perfect of a set-up.

When they walked back into the office, the same receptionist they'd spoken with on their first visit was there. She looked confused to see them again but not concerned.

"Well, hello again," she said. "Has there been any luck on your case?"

"Sadly, no," Jack said. "We feel like we might be making a bit of progress, though. And that progress led us to a man named Benjamin Lucas."

Rachel could see the recognition in her eyes. She nodded and seemed happy that she'd made the connection. "Oh, sure," she said. "He's our consultant for anyone that signs up for services. He makes sure all of the documentation and records are accurate and up to date."

"And not forged?" Rachel asked.

"Yes, and that, too."

"And does every single applicant see him?" Jack asked.

"Yes, at some point during the process. It's usually one of the very last things."

"So, in the case of Troy Hetfield, the latest name to be added to your waiting list, Dr. Lucas would have seen him within a few days of his murder, correct?"

Sheepishly, the receptionist said, "Yes."

"We need to speak with him, but he wasn't home," Jack said. "We thought he might be here."

"No, I'm sorry," she said. She looked at the laptop behind the desk and clicked around for a bit. "I'm looking on the schedule," she said, "and it shows that he has two in-home consults today. One of them is currently taking place."

"Are these new people for the waiting list?"

"I believe one of them is currently working to get on the list. The other…well, I can't give specific details, of course, but it's more of a check-up of sorts."

"We need to know the addresses of these homes," Rachel said.

"I'm very sorry, but I can't give you that information. Client confidentiality and all."

Rachel stepped forward, doing her best to keep her cool. "How well do you know Dr. Lucas?"

"Not very well. Just on a friendly basis when we pass each other at work."

"Well, you might be interested to know that Dr. Lucas is working for your foundation on a revoked license. And I can pretty much guarantee you that the people who run the foundation knew about this. So we can go through the proper channels and fill out forms and paperwork to get the information we need, or you can just give us the addresses. And if you go with the first option, Life Fulfilled is going to have some *very* bad press in the next week or so when Dr. Lucas's little secrets are revealed."

"I can't make that sort of decision. I'd have to call Mr.—"

"We don't have time for that right now," Jack pressed. "We need to speak with Dr. Lucas as soon as possible."

The receptionist was clearly flustered now, her eyes brimming with tears. She nodded, looking to the schedule and then to the laptop, then the phone, and then back to Rachel and Jack. "You don't have to say I gave it to you if it comes up later, do you?"

"No," Rachel said, though there was a chance that was a lie.

"He's currently seeing Vicki Freemont. The address is 1309 Jefferson Street."

"Thanks," Jack said, already turning to head for the door. Rachel followed and as she pushed her way through the door, she looked back to the receptionist one more time. She looked terrified and was quickly wiping a tear from her face. Rachel felt a brief rush of regret for how they'd bullied her but she didn't allow herself to dwell on it. Instead, she heaped it onto the rapidly growing pile of regrets and borderline-bad decisions she'd made in the past two days and decided to focus on the case instead. If she was taking this many risks to be a part of it, she supposed she needed to keep her mind focused on it at all costs.

***

The Freemont Street address was just fifteen minutes away from the Life Fulfilled offices. It was just off of one of the monument-lined cobblestone streets that etched their way through parts of Richmond's Fan District. Elms and sycamores lined the sidewalks, and the houses were almost all brick. When they parked on the opposite side of the street, Rachel spotted a small sedan with a Life Fulfilled decal on the driver's side door.

They walked up the little flagstone path to the front porch, which had several strands of ivy running up the brick posts. When Jack stepped forward to knock on the door, he made a very intentional effort to move in front of Rachel before she could do it. She understood it but couldn't deny that it stung a bit. Jack knocked and he got a response right away—though it wasn't quite the response either of them had been expecting.

It was a woman, presumably Vicki Freemont, screaming out in what sounded like a mix of pain and surprise. Rachel's instinct was to go inside even without anyone answering the door to make sure everything was okay. Jack, on the other hand, hammered on the door once more, calling out this time.

"Mrs. Freemont! Are you okay?"

There was no answer, but Rachel could hear the sound of something skidding across a floor, the sound of wood on wood, one of the objects falling over.

"Jack…" Rachel pleaded.

"Yeah, yeah."

He tried the doorknob and found it open. They rushed inside, Jack in the front and drawing his Glock as they went. Again, Rachel felt sorely out of place. No gun, no badge; she really was just a spectator at this point.

The front door opened up onto a foyer that instantly merged into a hallway. A den area lay to the right and a few other rooms interrupted the wall on the left. But it was at the end of the hall, in what looked to be a living room as they rushed to it, that the noise was coming from. Again, they heard a woman shout and this time, a man's murmuring voice behind it.

"It's okay, Mrs. Freemont," said a soothing male voice. "That's the worst of it. No more."

Rachel and Jack came to the living room and saw a woman of about fifty-five or sixty stretched out on a couch. An older man, easily seventy or so, sat on a small footstool beside the couch, checking the woman's blood pressure with the typical Velcro wrap and pump.

The older man saw them first, his eyes growing large when he saw Jack's gun. The woman saw his look of alarm and sat up.

"FBI agents," Jack said, slowly putting the Glock away. "We knocked in the door and no one answered."

The woman seemed very irritated, her thin lips creating a deep, intense frown. It made her look about twenty years older. "So you decided to barge on in with a gun drawn?"

"Ma'am," Rachel said, "we heard you screaming from the front porch."

"I'd say so. I've got a kidney that's barely functioning, and Dr. Lucas is kind of a bastard when it comes to taking blood pressure."

Lucas finally sized them up, turning to give them his full attention. He looked quite angry but Rachel saw clear signs of fear there as well—the shifting eyes, the overly rigid posture as he tried to make himself look stable and confident. "And why are you here, anyway? I'm on an in-home call to help care for Mrs. Freemont."

"Glad you asked, Dr. Lucas," Jack said. "We're actually here to speak with you."

"Is that right?" He spoke softly and glanced in Mrs. Freemont's direction. It was clear that he had a good idea why they might be here and he didn't want his patient to know.

"Yes, that's right," Rachel said. "And if you make things easy for us in these next few minutes, things may be easier than you'd imagine."

Mrs. Freemont sat up and made a strange, irritated huffing noise. "What the hell is this all about?"

"Sorry, ma'am," Jack said. "We just need to ask Dr. Lucas some questions."

"And it was so urgent that you had to come barreling in through my front door?"

"Actually, yes," Rachel said. "So, Dr. Lucas…do you have the time to speak with us?"

Lucas stared at Jack and Rachel for several seconds. It was like a game of chicken, both sides sizing the other up. As the seconds passed, Rachel could see his posture faltering and she could tell he was going to try to keep things civil. Killer or not a killer, he still had the very fragile remains of a reputation to keep in order.

"Here?" he asked.

Rachel thought it over for a moment and honestly saw no harm in staying in Mrs. Freemont's home. But before she could answer, Jack spoke up. "We'd rather not," he said. "We need to ask you questions pertaining to a sensitive case, and it would be better for all parties involved if it was done at the bureau offices."

Rachel reached out and lightly tugged at his sleeve. He'd clearly forgotten that there was no way she could go to the field office right now—not when she was supposed to be on a two-week leave of absence.

"I don't underst—" Lucas started, but then went quiet. He looked to Mrs. Freemont one last time before focusing solely on the agents.

Jack seemed to finally get the clue, though. He sighed, clearly frustrated at the situation, and shrugged. He then swerved things and used their current situation to come off as an understanding and likeable agent.

"Fine, we don't have to take you to the office—yet. But due to the sensitive nature of the case, we'll step outside. Mrs. Freemont, are we okay to use your porch?"

She frowned, adjusting her weight on the couch as if she simply could not get comfortable. "If you must."

Rachel saw the ease and comfort that rose up in Lucas's eyes. It threw Rachel off a bit. He hadn't been out and out defiant about going to the FBI offices, which spoke of either a resigned form of guilt or simple agreeability. Or, of course, it could simply be a ruse to confuse them. This was a man operating without a medical license, after all; there was no telling how far he might go to cover himself. So really, the fact that they were keeping things to a minimum and not officially taking him in might end up playing in their favor. The comfort and lackadaisical nature of it all could easily cause him to slip up.

"We're good here, Mrs. Freemont," Lucas said. "I'll give your results to Life Fulfilled and they'll work with your doctor to ensure the best decisions are made."

Mrs. Freemont only nodded, clearly disgruntled by the sudden interruption to her day. He then nodded to Jack and Rachel and, with a strange look of acceptance on his face, gestured to the hallway. Jack started forward, and Rachel bookended them, coming in behind Lucas. As they exited Vicki Freemont's home, Rachel couldn't help but feel as if Dr. Lucas was leading them along rather than the other way around.

CHAPTER NINETEEN

It wasn't until they sat down on Mrs. Freemont's porch that Rachel realized that Dr. Lucas reminded her a bit of Alex Lynch. He seemed unflappable and somehow in control of his thoughts, emotions, and faculties even in the face of potential trouble. Lucas's hair, which was almost a total shade of white, eerily resembled Lynch's as well. Lastly, though, it was the way the man looked at the world. His eyes seemed to hardly blink and he stared at things—passing cars on the street, the back of Jack's head, the little glider-style rocket he sat down in on the porch—as if he were trying to study every feature.

Lucas did not put up a fight, nor did he argue or complain as he sat down and waited for whatever they had to talk about. He was remarkably cool and collected, something that made Rachel feel slightly uneasy.

"Dr. Lucas, before we get into our reasons for needing to speak with you today," Rachel said, "I'd like for you to tell us what happened in Tennessee. We know why you lost your license, but we'd like to hear your side of things."

He gave a little shrug, as if they were talking about some mild crime, maybe a parking ticket or something insubstantial. "If you read about it and know about it, there's nothing I can add. I screwed up a morphine dosage and it killed my patient."

"Triple the usual amount doesn't seem like a mistake that a practiced doctor would make," Jack said.

"You're absolutely right. But in my defense, I had been sleeping poorly and this patient was having some of the worst pain symptoms I'd ever seen. Bone cancer with osteoarthritis thrown in for a sick little bonus. Did you happen to read *that* in your research? The screams of agony this woman would belt out gave me nightmares. She begged for death daily and even fought for medically assisted suicide, but as I'm sure you know, that's a very touchy subject."

"Was this your way of giving in to her wishes?" Rachel asked.

"Absolutely not," he said, showing real emotion for the first time since they'd arrived. "Oh, there were days where it crossed my mind, but those thoughts were fleeting and selfish. But no...as I told the courts and the jury, it was a terrible mistake on my part. I wasn't paying attention, I was tired, and the trauma of it all was just…it was gut-wrenching. There was never enough evidence to even begin to argue against any of this. That's why having my license stripped was the only punishment. No jail time, no fines."

"When did you move to Virginia?" Jack asked.

"About three years ago. I moved here specifically to start working with Life Fulfilled. There are other organizations and foundations that do the same thing, but they are very personal and relatable. They really go the extra mile to make sure their clients are treated like real people rather than fragile little death-sentences."

"And they had no issue with your past in Tennessee?" Rachel asked.

"Of course they did," he said. More emotion was climbing into his voice and she couldn't help but wonder how many more blunt questions might make him transform completely. "It was a very heated conversation and I nearly didn't get the job."

"So tell us how this works, exactly," Rachel said. "You have no license, so how are you on staff as a medical doctor?"

Lucas drew in a deep breath and when he let it out, he seemed to deflate, as if he were a balloon someone had stuck with a pin. "It comes down to technicality," he said. "In the course of my time with Life Fulfilled I have not once, not a single time, practiced medicine. The overwhelming majority of my job comes down to checking records and simply giving opinions on the well-being of clients."

"You were taking Mrs. Freemont's blood pressure when we came in," Jack pointed out.

Lucas's mouth thinned into something that was part grimace and part grin. "That's again a technicality. Either of you could go to any pharmacy right now and buy a low-quality blood pressure cuff. And anyone that's been to the doctor a single time or knows how to run a Google search can figure out how to take the reading. I've also taken blood, for the record—something anyone with basic nursing knowledge can do, as is evidenced in the multiple blood drives in this area every year."

Damn, he's good, Rachel thought. It was quite clear he had this argument at the ready at all times. She was pretty sure he'd had to explain it numerous times based on the ease of delivery.

Jack glanced over at Rachel as he sat forward in one of the other chairs on the porch. She gave him a nod, indicating she, too, thought it was time to go ahead and show their hand. Given how practiced and calm he now seemed to be, his facial expressions might go a long way to letting them know his level of involvement in these recent murders. Rachel wasn't sure if she thought he was their man yet, but she was not at all convinced he was *not*.

Let me tell you why we came to speak with you, Dr. Lucas," Jack said. "We've been speaking with Life Fulfilled in regards to a case we're working on. So far, three people on their waiting list have been murdered. Being that the waiting list and recent terminal illnesses are the only links between them, it is very likely that the killer has access to the Life Fulfilled waiting list. Take that circumstance and set it next to your history and maybe you can see why you'd be a person of interest."

As Jack spelled everything out to him, Rachel watched Lucas's face. It remained fairly stable and flat up until Jack mentioned the link of terminal illnesses and the Life Fulfilled waiting list. He didn't look simply shocked; he looked mortified.

"How…how long has this been going on?" Lucas asked.

"Five days," Jack said.

"I can assure you that I have nothing to do with it. If you…" He stopped and did his best to gain control of his thoughts. "If you can tell me when these murders supposedly occurred, I will do my very best to give you my location at the time." He looked to both of them with shame in his eyes. When he looked away, down to his hands, Rachel saw a single tear race down his face, leaving a thin, wet trail. "I understand why you'd think I could, though. With what happened all those years ago…I get it. But I've lived with that for so long—and this job with Life Fulfilled is supposed to be my way to make up for it. To right that awful wrong."

"You speak about it as if you knew what you were doing back then," Jack said. "That it wasn't really a mistake."

"She begged me," Lucas said, matter-of-factly. "She begged me several times to help her slip away. She asked me to not tell her when, but to maybe up her meds, maybe do something that would put her peacefully under. I…I spoke with her therapist and we tried to figure out the morality of it all. I don't know that I ever flat out ignored the idea. It was always there in the back of my mind. I suppose I could have subconsciously done it…maybe convincing myself that I had made a mistake. I just don't…I don't *think* so. But either way, I did not kill her."

Once again, Rachel and Jack shared a look and a nearly telepathic thought. This time, it was Rachel who spoke it out loud. "We're going to need you to give us a pretty accurate detailed schedule of your whereabouts over the past five days," she said. "After that, you're free to go, but we'll need you to not leave town until your alibis have checked out."

"I understand. I do have to ask, though—and I hope you'll forgive me. But Life Fulfilled isn't going to take any dings because of my involvement, are they? Once you find out I'm clear of this, does anything need to be said about my past in the public eye?"

"I don't see why not," Jack said. "That's between you and Life Fulfilled. So long as you aren't actively practicing medicine, I don't see where any laws are being broken."

"Thank you," Lucas said, looking genuinely grateful. And then, slowly and as if to make sure he didn't leave out a single detail, Dr. Lucas started to give a very deep breakdown of his past week or so. Within a few seconds, Rachel started to feel certain he was innocent. He was giving too many details and exact names and times for it to be a line of bullshit. This number of details would certainly lay several traps for anyone who was lying.

She watched as Jack took down notes and names, the humbled look on his face indicating that he was also coming to the conclusion that this was not their man. She also knew, though, that Jack had the assurance of knowing that he could go right to work on digging up new leads and he could do it without any real hindrance. As for her, the fact that they were questioning Lucas on Mrs. Freemont's porch was a clear indicator of what sort of hoops she was going to have to jump through to stay on the case.

The easy solution, she knew, was to just go back home and let Jack handle it. He was fully capable, after all. But she knew that was wishful thinking. Not only was she in too deep to turn away now, she was starting to take the case personally. Someone was out there killing people based on bad bills of health—people who had committed no wrongs other than being dealt a very bad hand when it came to their health. To say that she could sympathize with these victims was an understatement. And she fully intended to ride this case out until the end, no matter what the consequences might be.

CHAPTER TWENTY

He ate a fast-food burger as he watched the red Ford Explorer pull out of the pharmacy parking lot. There were two people in the Explorer—his next victim and someone he assumed was the victim's caregiver. According to the list, this victim was Brittany Neal, sixty-eight years of age. He'd selected her at random from the list and had worried that her age might make her a little harder to get to than the other three he'd taken so far.

He'd staked her out here and there over the past two days and was finding that he may have to skip her. If things went perfectly, he'd come back to her but for right now, it seemed like too much trouble, and too much time to put into one single person. Still, he'd come this far so he figured he may as well follow the Explorer back to her home, just a mile or so away from the pharmacy.

He made sure not to follow too closely because it seemed safe. But really, he doubted the driver would be too worried about the possibility of being followed. Even if they had it on their radar, surely they were too focused on Brittany Neal to keep an eye out for such things. When the Explorer turned into the concrete driveway of a two-story home in an affluent neighborhood, he kept driving by. He watched in his rearview as the car parked in a garage attached to the west wing of the house. He thought he also saw another car parked in the small, rectangular driveway.

He came to the end of the street and made a U-turn—not a difficult feat at one in the afternoon. He drove back by the house and confirmed that there *was* another car in the driveway. It was a black Acura, the same car he'd seen there yesterday. As far as he knew, it hadn't moved. Also, when he'd come by yesterday, there had been several other visitors at the house as well.

Given Mrs. Neal's age and the number of visitors she seemed to keep at her home he couldn't help but wonder if she might be in her final days. And if that were the case, he was pretty sure there would be a constant influx of people coming in and out of her home over the course of those days—however many more there may be.

It was disappointing, but not enough to get him off-course. He passed by her house as he finished off his burger, drove several streets over and parked inside a random office park. He had the waiting list saved to his phone, so he opened it up and read it over. There honestly wasn't a lot of information on the list, just enough to get him started: client name, client age, name of the person that filled out the application, and, in some cases, the client's address. One thing he was beginning to note was that it was typically the ones who filled out their own applications that were the easiest to approach. From what he could tell, these were people who were usually on their own, with no family or real support systems around them. At first, he was surprised to also find that this was overwhelmingly the sort of person who signed up for the services that Life Fulfilled offered. But the more he came to understand these people, the more it made sense; if there were loved ones surrounding you, there was a lesser chance you'd actually need to go to such lengths as to seek services from a foundation like Life Fulfilled. It was those who were on their own that seemed to come to them the most.

There was no real rhyme or reason to how he selected his victims. It was almost like a playful game of choice. Even now, he ran a ketchup-smeared finger down the screen of his phone, stopping it at random. The name he was pointing to was Donna Kelley. She was forty-nine and had filled out her information herself. She lived roughly twelve miles away from where he was currently parked, but that was fine. It wasn't like he had anything else to do this afternoon.

He studied the address one more time and set his phone down. He wasn't being so brazen as to attack the victims in their homes. In such enclosed spaces, he knew there was a much higher risk of leaving behind clues in the form of loose hairs or footprints. It also seemed that just about everyone had a camera-driven doorbell now, too. Still, starting at their homes was a good way to track them and learn about their comings and goings. And when they posted things on social media, that helped a great deal, too.

He pulled out of the office park and got back out onto the highway. Though he was in no rush, he still found himself speeding. While he may not have any sort of timeframe to work within, most of the people on this list *did* have a limited amount of time. And if they were on a clock, then he supposed he was, too.

It was a strange and almost ironic thought that had him grinning as he drove in the direction of what he thought might very well turn out to be his fourth victim.

CHAPTER TWENTY ONE

Within ten minutes of leaving Vicki Freemont's house, Rachel could tell that Jack was heading in the direction of her house. When he turned onto Broad Street and headed in the direction of downtown rather than the interstate and the direction of the field office, it was quite clear. She supposed she really couldn't argue. After a certain point, she really became nothing more than a hindrance to him. He was having to be careful about certain things he said on the phone and it wasn't like he could just roll up to the field office with her in tow.

As she thought through all of this, Jack spoke up, admitting something that Rachel had also been thinking about but didn't want to face. "With Lucas not fitting the bill and now with no new leads of any kind, we're going to have to go the police custody route for every single person remaining on that wait list."

"Anderson will have an aneurysm," she said.

"Likely. But I think he'll also understand. I mean, it's sort of a godsend that we even have a list of people that could be potential victims. It's a hell of a lot easier than having the entire city wide open as a pool of potential victims."

Rachel thought back to a case from earlier in her career where she'd had to orchestrate a similar task. For that case, it had only been seven people who needed protecting and it had been like pulling teeth. With more than twenty people needing police protection, it was going to be a nightmare for manpower and scheduling.

"There's no way that's going to be possible by the end of the day," Rachel said. "And all it's going to do is make the killer harder to find anyway. If he's out on the hunt and notices that police presence…"

"I thought of that, too, but we can't just keep those people out there unprotected, using them as bait," Jack said. "I wonder if there's anything Life Fulfilled can do—maybe something Wes Dalton can do. Make calls to each person and have them or their loved ones keep an eye out. That and maybe just a heightened police presence in their communities rather than full-blown protective custody and stakeouts."

As he said this, an idea came to Rachel. It was a long shot, but one she thought they were desperate enough to try. "Yesterday, didn't the receptionist at Life Fulfilled say Dalton should be back today?"

"She did," Jack confirmed.

"When you were charming her socks off, did you happen to get his number?"

"I did, actually." As they came to a stoplight, he reached into the breast pocket of his coat. "You think it's even worth calling him?"

"Can't hurt. He knows we're in the middle of an investigation that has his foundation in its center and he's not bothered calling. Sure, he *could* just be busy. But it also feels like he's trying to dodge or hide. And coming from a man who willingly and knowingly hired a doctor that had his medical license revoked makes it seem even fishier."

She reached out for the business card. As Jack handed it over, he looked at her skeptically. "This wouldn't just be a brilliant ploy to try to get me to keep you on this case for a bit longer, would it?"

Rather than answer, she simply shrugged as she typed Wes Dalton's number into her phone. She placed the call on speaker mode and set it on the armrest between the driver and passenger seats. After the third ring, Rachel was fully expecting it to go to voicemail, so she was surprised when it was answered midway through the fourth.

"Hello?" Wes Dalton said on the other end. He wasn't necessarily speaking in a whisper, but his voice was very low and almost raspy.

"Is this Wes Daltron, chairman of Life Fulfilled?" Rachel asked.

"Yes, it is. And who is this?"

"This is Special Agent Rachel Gift. My partner, Jack Rivers, is also on the line."

"Yes, I was told there were FBI agents in our offices asking questions. And I do want to help but as I'm sure you were told I'm in New York."

"We were also told that you'd be back today," Rachel said.

"That was the plan, yes. But things changed a bit and now I don't fly out until tomorrow morning."

"You didn't find it pressing to come in to represent your foundation when you know there are people on your waiting list that are being killed?"

"Coming in tomorrow is the best I can do under the circumstances," he said. "If there was anything I could do to be there sooner, I would."

"And you're at a conference, correct?"

"Yes, I am."

"What conference is it?"

"It's a seminar on end of life practices. Best approaches and practices to assist those in their final days."

"Are you speaking?"

"No, just visiting and taking in some of the curriculums. Listen, I need to get back. There's a round table I'm supposed to be a part of. But you have my word. As soon as I get back tomorrow, I'll get in touch. Is this the number I should all?"

"Yes, it is," Rachel said, instantly suspicious. "When does your plane leave in the morning?"

"I'm not too sure, actually. I don't have the reservation information in front of me. I believe it was ten o'clock, though."

"Okay. So we'll expect your call tomorrow." She noticed Jack looking at her with confused eyes, as if to ask her: *That's it? Really?*

"Yes, absolutely," Dalton said.

Rachel hung up and instantly opened up Google. She typed in *conferences, New York City, medical, psychology,* and then the day's date. As the results came up, she heard Jack chuckling from the driver's seat. "Checking up on him?"

"Sure am."

"You think he's lying?"

"Sure do."

She got three relevant hits based on her results. One was for a sports medicine clinic that was being put on by the NCAA. Another was a symposium that discussed the use of low-grade hallucinogenics on patients suffering from depression, and the other was specifically for cardiologists who were focusing on heart disease.

"Nothing here checks out," she said. She then pulled up her Flights app and checked for all flights leaving New York City and arriving in Richmond, Virginia, tomorrow morning. There was one at 8:12 and the next closest one was 1:45. There were more between these two, but the destinations were Charlotte, NC, and Washington, DC—neither of which really made sense unless he was landing in DC and then driving to Richmond.

"See what you can do about finding his location based on the GPS on his phone," Rachel said. She knew it was not only possible but that the bureau was getting better at these types of things, often getting results within half an hour.

"Seems a little aggressive," Jack said.

"So does killing people based on the fact that they have terminal illnesses," she pointed out."

She listened as Jack made the call while she double-checked on the conferences she'd searched. She even opened up the search terms to any conferences and conventions at all. The number increased significantly but nothing was geared to patients at the end of their lives.

Jack ended his call as she made her way through the list, passing by a comic book convention.

"Why would he lie about being in New York?" Jack wondered out loud.

"It's a good question, but an even *better* question when you place it next to the fact that he's got clients being murdered while he's away. The timing simply doesn't look very good for him."

Jack nodded his agreement, giving his turn signal and pulling over into a shopping center parking lot. They were about seven miles from her house, so the move made her assume Jack was wanting to see how this all played out before he took her back home. And though she knew Paige would be home in a little under two hours, Rachel did not feel that sense of a ticking clock like she did yesterday. If there was any ticking clock at all, it was in regards to the case.

"It *would* make sense," Jack said. "Let's say he *is* the killer. If this trace comes back to show that he's actually not in New York, that he's still here in Richmond, that seems almost perfect, right? Maybe he's been coming up with all manner of excuses so that he can go out and kill these people on his waiting list—a list that he's not going to have any problem getting his hands on because he's the one that oversees it." He gave a nervous laugh and said, "Damn, he *does* seem like a likely candidate when you boil it down like that."

"That's along the lines of what I was thinking." She was going to offer some more insight but she was interrupted by the sound of her phone ringing. Jack jumped a bit, reaching for his own, but stopped when he realized it was Rachel's. The display told her it was Grandma Tate and her first thought was that something was wrong at school— that Paige had gotten sick. That, or maybe Grandma Tate's cancer had come back.

Her nerves started to fire and spark as she answered the call. "Hello?"

"Rachel…hello."

"Is everything okay?"

"Oh, yes. Perfectly fine. I was just wondering if you planned to be home after I pick Paige up from school."

Rachel wasn't sure, but she thought there might be a bit of accusation to the question. And while Rachel honestly didn't blame her, it stung all the same. "I doubt it. But I should be home in time for dinner, unless something big comes up."

"I see…"

"Is that okay? Do you need me to come home?"

There was no response for a while but after giving a sigh, Grandma Tate answered and this time, there was no doubt that there was some accusation behind it. "I'm not here to tell you how to live the rest of your life," she said. "But I *will* say this: I love Paige to pieces and I don't mind spending all of this time with her. But I did not decide to temporarily move in so that you could continue to go off and try to work yourself to your very last breath. I came to help you along in your time of need. But right now, if I'm being perfectly honest, I feel like you're using my presence as another excuse to just retreat back to work."

It all took Rachel a bit off guard. She didn't think Grandma Tate had ever spoken to her like this. It made her feel like a little girl who had just gotten in trouble but it also made her feel deeply ashamed…and a little angry.

"Retreat?" she asked, finding it odd that of the entire lecture, that was the word that had hurt the most. She also became very aware that Jack was in the car with her, doing his best to occupy himself with his own phone and not get involved.

"Well, let's be honest, dear. That's what you're doing. You're afraid to slow down at work because you'll have to actually face what's coming your way and process it. I just thought you'd want to process it while spending time with your daughter."

Rachel almost said, *"That's not fair,"* but bit the response back. After all, she supposed it kind of *was* the truth. Apparently, Grandma Tate sensed that Rachel's silence was an indicator that her point was made.

"I'll let Paige know you might be late. Goodbye, Rachel."

Rachel did her best to keep her composure as she tucked her phone back into her pocket. It was an odd feeling to be filled with anger while also feeling her heart breaking a bit. She imagined Grandma Tate telling Paige that her mother would be late coming home again. Yes, even after sharing the news of her bad health and looming death, and yes even after her father had walked out on them, Mommy was choosing work. She was choosing to *retreat* to her work.

She found it hard to look at Jack, knowing what she had to say. She needed him to take her home. She needed him to—

Jack's phone rang and he answered it right away. The look on his face as he brought the phone to his face told her that he was very glad the tension of her personal problems filling the car was broken.

"This is Agent Rivers," he answered. He did not set this all to speaker, maybe assuming she needed time to process the conversation she'd just had. She listened to him give a few *uh-huh*s to whoever was on the other line and then a quick *Thanks* as he ended the call.

"Was that an update?" she asked him.

"It was. And I hate to say it, but it seems you were right. The bureau ran a trace on Wes Dalton's phone and it turns out he wasn't in New York. Not even close."

"Then where is he?"

"At a hotel…right here in Richmond. And from what they can tell, he's been there for at least two days."

Though it was a no-brainer for Rachel to remain with Jack for this sudden break, the guilt came at full force, too. *This has to be it for today,* Rachel told herself. *After we check this lead out, it's back home to Paige.*

But even then, she knew it might be a difficult promise to keep. What if this lead led to another, then to another? Where did she draw the line?

She didn't know. And in that moment, as they raced to the hotel, Rachel was a bit worried that she couldn't even *see* that line anymore.

CHAPTER TWENTY TWO

The hotel was a simple little Best Western, located on the opposite side of the city. As Jack made the drive over, Rachel was again filled with conflicting feelings: relief from being pulled away from the truths Grandma Tate had dropped on her, and regret because she was electing to stay on the case. She understood that there was a bit of conceit to what she was doing—the feeling that the case could only be brought to a satisfying close if she was on it. She knew if she dug a bit deeper, the truth of the matter was that her daughter needed her at home a hell of a lot more than Jack needed her to help close out this case. But that, of course, was yet another truth she was not ready to face.

Jack pulled the car into the parking lot, taking up a spot right in front of the office. "All I got was the address," he told Rachel as they got out of the car. "Of course, tracking the phone wasn't nearly specific enough to give us a room number."

"Well, I very seriously doubt he checked in under his real name," Rachel said.

"Yeah, doubtful. We'll just have to hope to get lucky."

They walked inside the office where a middle-aged woman was typing something into her phone. She looked up to them and smiled as they approached the desk. "Good afternoon," she said. "You folks need a room?"

"No, thanks," Jack said, showing his badge. "We're Agents Rivers and Gift, with the FBI. We've traced a suspect's phone to this hotel and are hoping he used his real name to check in."

The woman turned her attention immediately to the desktop monitor in front of her. She looked very stern and serious, anxious to help the FBI. "What's the name?"

"Wes Dalton."

She typed the name in and shook her head. "No such name. Hold on…I can check to see if that name comes up on any credit card transactions. Do you know when he would have checked in?"

"No," Jack said. "We just know he's been here for at least the last two days."

The woman nodded and clicked away at the keyboard. After a few more seconds, she scrolled with the mouse, scanning the screen.

"Nothing. But if he used a fake name, which some people do because…well, affairs and all, he probably paid cash. And as far as I know, there have only been four or five rooms that were paid with cash in the past two days. And all but one of them checked out earlier today." She glanced to the monitor again and added: "This morning, in fact."

"So there's one more guest currently staying here that paid cash?" Rachel asked.

"That's right. Room 27. They gave the name of Allison Kelvin."

The name seemed familiar, but Rachel didn't waste time trying to figure it out. Jack thanked the receptionist and they headed out, taking the first flight of stairs on the outside of the building and making their way to the walkway along the second floor. It was the sort of hotel where the doors were all exposed to the open air, the concrete walkways covered only by the underside of the walkway above them.

They came to the door of room 27 and paused outside. Jack took a steadying breath and knocked. Perhaps, Rachel thought, he had the same feeling she did—of knowing that one way or the other, they were about to step into a pivotal moment for the case.

There was a space of roughly three seconds between the knock and their response. It was a woman's voice, presumably Allison Kelvin. "Yes, who's there?"

The woman sounded tired and out of sorts. Hearing her voice seemed to help Rachel make the connection. She suddenly understood why the name seemed so familiar.

"Agent Rivers, with the FBI," Jack said. Once he'd gotten that out of the way, Rachel leaned in closer, whispering in his ear. "Allison Kelvin is a name on the Life Fulfilled waiting list."

Jack stared at the door, waiting for a response, his eyes narrowed and focused. "Is this Ms. Kelvin?" he asked through the door.

Again, there were several seconds before he got an answer. Rachel could imagine her inside the room, formulating an answer that would pacify them. Or being given an answer by someone else in the room.

"It is. And I'm not feeling well," she finally answered.

"Ma'am, I need you to open the door."

Jack's hand went to his Glock. Rachel understood the impulse, as the fact that there was a woman on the waiting list inside a room they highly suspected Wes Dalton to have rented out was beyond suspicious.

"No. I'm not feeling well and I need you to go away."

"I assure you, it's for your own safety. Now, I ask that you stand back because if you aren't going to open this door, I'm going to kick it down."

"That's highly uncalled for!"

"You have three seconds, ma'am."

Rachel stepped to the side, giving Jack enough room to get some sort of momentum from the thin area of the walkway between the door and the rail of the walkway. He nodded to her and started counting.

"One. Two. Th—"

"Hold your damned horses!" Allison yelled from inside the room.

The sound of a chain coming unlocked from a clasp could be heard, followed by the hollow-sounding *thunk* of the door's lock being disengaged. Jack relaxed a bit, his hand coming away from his Glock as he started to take a step forward.

The door was pulled open quickly and before either Jack or Rachel was fully aware of what was happening, someone came rushing out. All Rachel could tell for certain at first was that it was a man. He came barreling out of the room, directly toward Jack. The two men collided, sending Jack stumbling backwards to the iron rail behind him. As he struck it, the man turned to the right, in Rachel's direction. He was still moving quickly, head lowered and shoulders just starting to come up from his attack on Jack.

He saw Rachel at the very last moment. Not expecting a second person, the man hesitated for just a moment. Rachel braced herself as he continued forward. She lowered her own shoulder and assumed a position very much like a linebacker. The man didn't barge into her with the same force he's used on Jack; the hesitation made him slower and weaker. The result was Rachel easily being able to stop him, thrusting her shoulder into his chest and sending him down to the concrete in an awkward tackle.

The man cried out as Rachel pushed herself up, driving a knee into his chest. Knowing she had no cuffs on her, she could only wait for Jack to scramble over. Jack helped flip the man over onto his stomach as he wrenched his cuffs from his belt.

"What's your name, sir?" Jack asked.

The man said nothing. He wasn't fighting against them and though he grunted and moaned a bit at the harsh actions Jack took in pulling his arms behind his back, he also wasn't very verbal. Rachel also noticed a woman standing just inside of the doorway, making a few tiny steps further back into the room. One hand was at her heart and the other was covering her mouth in shock. She was a pretty woman of about thirty-five or so. Her hair was perfectly blonde and she had a fairly perfect figure. She watched the entire scene unfold with tired blue eyes.

"Wes Dalton?" Rachel asked.

"Yes," the man grunted.

This confirmation seemed to put a bit more urgency and anger into how Jack handled the man. He yanked Dalton to his feet and pushed him into the room. "Sit your ass on the bed," Jack said.

Wes Dalton did as he was asked. He was bleeding slightly from a cut on the chin but his gaze seemed cool and unaffected. He looked to the woman apologetically and then back to Jack.

Rachel walked over to the woman. "You're Allison Kelvin?"

"Yes."

"And recently, you've been placed on the waiting list for Life fulfilled, correct?"

Allison only nodded this time, as if she were ashamed.

"Leave her alone," Dalton said. It was the first thing out of his mouth since he'd come rushing through the door, trying to make a run for it. "You can ask me all the questions."

Ignoring him, Rachel kept her gaze focused on Allison. She nearly asked Allison if Dalton had been here to kill her. But then she saw the state of the bed, in disarray. The bathroom door behind Allison was partly open and she could see a pair of boxer briefs on the floor. A bra was also hanging from the towel rack. And though Allison was currently dressed in a T-shirt and a pair of shorts, the messy state of her hair made it clear that Dalton had not been here to kill her. Judging from the two separate bags packed over by the other side of the room, Rachel started to assume quite the opposite, actually.

"Fine then," Rachel said, directing her gaze back to Dalton. "We can start with the most obvious question: why did you lie about going to New York?"

"You *do* know why we're here, right?" Jack asked.

"Same reason you gave when you called me, I suppose," Dalton said. There were nerves in his voice but it was clear he was trying to remain in control, not wanting to seem as if he might cower in front of them at any moment. "You want to know about the people on the waiting list. Wanting to ask me questions about the foundation."

"Oh, it's not quite that simple," Jack said. "You lied about where you were and why you were there. That's bad enough, but this lie, if believed, conveniently kept you away from Richmond while people on your waiting list were being killed. Can you follow the bread crumbs, or do I need to spell it out for you?"

He did look confused for a moment, but then the realization of what Jack was saying settled in his eyes. He leaned back on the bed, his cuffed arms behind his back nearly making him fall over. "You think I'm killing these people? Why in God's name would I do that?"

"It's a good question," Jack said. "And it's the *main* question we want to ask you."

"Well, there's another one," Rachel said. "And I think that one answers itself by a quick glance around the room. Which of you wants to clear up what's going on here?"

"I will," Dalton said. "Allison has been through enough. Just leave her alone."

"I'm so sorry, Wes," Allison said, standing by the bathroom door. She was crying, unable to take her eyes away from Dalton.

"Allison came into the office about four months ago," Dalton started. "I didn't actually meet her until about a month or so into the process. She's been diagnosed with chronic lymphocytic leukemia. The doctors have given her another seven months. She could maybe beat it, but she's already beaten breast cancer, so her body is very weak."

"He was so caring, so kind," Allison spoke up. "Wes and everyone at Life Fulfilled treated me like any other human being, not just some poor woman who is going to die much sooner than she should."

"There was something between us right from the start," Dalton said. "And after the second time we met, I crossed a line I knew I shouldn't. I stopped by her house one afternoon on my way home. I used the lame excuse of needing a form signed. She invited me in for coffee and that was it."

"We were hooked," Allison said.

"So we've been spending as much time together as we can," Dalton said. "And I'm sure you can imagine how bad it would look if the founder of Life Fulfilled was found to be having a romantic relationship with someone on the waiting list. I offered several times to bump her to the top, but she's refused every single time."

"Is this the first time you've lied about your schedule to create time for the two of you?" Jack asked.

He shook his head and looked longingly at Allison. "No. This has got to at least be the third or fourth. I did it last month; said I was going to be gone for four days for a training exercise so Allison and I could spend a weekend at an Airbnb in the Blue Ridge Mountains."

"He says there are people on the waiting list being killed?" Allison said.

"Yes, there are," Rachel said. She then directed her attention to Dalton and added: "And unless you can provide proof or alibis for your whereabouts over the last five days, you're considered a suspect."

"Well, for the last two days, I've been in this room with Allison. The only time I left was to go down to Allison's car to get a phone charger. After…Jesus, after I learned that people on the waiting list were being killed, I was afraid to leave her alone, you know?"

"He's right," Allison said. She gave him what Rachel thought was supposed to be a cute, suggestive grin. "He's been in here with me for almost two whole days."

Many comments came to Rachel's mind but she clamped down on them. Chief among them was: *So you just let the others on the waiting list languish while you were sleeping with this woman?*

"And what about the three before that?" Jack asked.

Dalton thought for a moment, forcing himself to look beyond the blissful snag of this hotel room and the days that came before it. "Three days ago…I worked in the morning and played golf with an investor after lunch. That night, I visited Allison at her house."

"You worked from the office that morning?" Jack asked.

"Yes. Two others were there and can vouch for me."

"Who'd you golf with?"

"An older gentleman named Maxwell Forbes and one of his assistants. We had a few drinks at the clubhouse bar afterwards, and there were at least a dozen other people there that can confirm this."

"And the two days before that?" Rachel asked.

"Two days ago, I was in DC, having a few meetings. I was going to stay the night but came home late. The next day I went to work and I was there all day. Well into the night, actually, getting ready for the three days I planned to spend with Allison."

With every sentence he spoke, Rachel could feel the hope of closing the case slipping farther and farther away. There were too many specifics to his story, and far too many people to verify his location during each murder.

"We're going to have agents look into these alibis and stories," Jack said. His tone had softened, and Rachel could tell that he believed every word of what Dalton had said. "In the meantime, you go nowhere. It's either this motel room, work, or your home, do you understand? If we get so much as a hint that you're on the move, you *will* be brought in as a primary suspect."

"Yeah, I got that," Dalton said. "Understood."

Rachel could feel the disappointment oozing off of Jack as they both took one last look around the room. Dalton was a miserable and wretched man, but he was far from a killer. They made their exit, closing the door behind them. Rachel looked down to the concrete where she'd tackled Wes Dalton and saw a small smear of blood from where he'd nicked his chin.

"You know," Jack said as they made their way back to the car, "that would almost be a sweet story…what's going on with Allison and Wes Dalton. But the murders sort of put a damper on it, you know?"

They'd reached the car and Rachel was reaching out for the door handle on the passenger side when her phone rang. She grabbed for it right away, wondering if it might be Grandma Tate, calling to apologize for her earlier outburst. But when she saw DIR. ANDERSON on her caller display, her heart felt like it was seizing up in her chest.

"Shit," she hissed. "It's Anderson."

"Do you think he knows you're with me somehow?"

"I don't know." And in saying that, she started to wonder if she'd really even give a damn. He may slap her on the wrist and chew her out, but what was the worst he could say, really? Despite this hopeful realization, she still found herself rather afraid to answer the call. When she finally answered, she felt the stirrings of a headache in the back of her head. It came in a low, bass-like rumble at the very top of her head and started to spread right away.

"This is Agent Gift," she said, answering in a professional way without realizing she was doing so.

"Agent Gift," Anderson said, his voice level and somehow serene. "I've just gotten an update from the US Marshals on the hunt for Alex Lynch and I thought you'd want to be filled in. It seems that the trail has gone cold. They've got a number of leads and there are still about a dozen bodies on it but it's not looking good."

Rachel felt like she'd been punched right in the stomach. The wind went out of her and for a moment, the world was reeling. She thought of Lynch out there, God only knew where, actually, and just as free as anyone else. She could only hope the maniac was headed down to Aiken, South Carolina. He'd sent Grandma Tate mail there so it stood to reason that would be where he was headed. Of course, the US Marshals would have already considered that and—

"Rachel? You there?" Anderson said. His voice sounded far away and ghostly.

"Yes, sir. I'm here. I just…nothing. Thanks for the call."

Before he could say or ask anything else, she hung up.

"What did he want?" Jack asked as he opened the car.

"To let me know the trail on Lynch is going cold pretty damned quick. He said—"

She stopped as that low-thrumming headache seemed to expand. It felt as if it had tendrils that were reaching out into her head. It didn't hurt all that bad honestly, but it came on fast. It was so fast that the world continued to reel as it had when she'd answered the call from Anderson. She leaned against the car for support but even that wasn't enough.

"Rachel?" It was Jack's voice, but very distorted.

No…I was doing so well, she thought. *Just a few hours ago, I was marveling over how I hadn't felt so well since getting the diagnosis.*

She felt the car slipping away from her and after that, she was falling. She braced for the impact, but the world had gone black before she felt it.

CHAPTER TWENTY THREE

She was dreaming of her honeymoon in Martha's Vineyard. Peter's grandfather had owned a house out there and it was a place she'd always wanted to visit. For five entire days, she'd had a grand view of the Atlantic Ocean and had paid waitstaff to tend to her every need. She'd lost count of how many times she and Peter had made love, both of them fully okay with possibly finding out in just a few weeks that they were already expecting.

It hadn't happened then, of course. It had taken a few years for her to get pregnant and when Paige had come, it had been exactly what they'd both wanted. She'd watched Peter melt at the very moment he first held his daughter. He'd not cried or wept, but melted; he'd become this totally different thing, some emotional mass that seemed somehow more than human in that moment.

But the honeymoon…that was the picture that had fastened itself into her mind. There had been a moment on the third morning when she'd woken up long before Peter. She'd stepped outside on the large wraparound porch with nothing but a thin sheet wrapped around her. She'd stared out to the ocean, listening to the crashing waves against the soft purples and oranges of a dawn backdrop. Listening to the ocean, she'd closed her eyes and dared to dream what the future might be like. A loving husband, a child, a job she was already on the way toward, watching her child graduate from high school, and then college, and then one day holding her grandchildren. She's seen it all clearly on that morning and it had felt so real and chilling that she had so doubt that it would all come true exactly the way she saw it.

Slowly, that image faded. Only the sound of the ocean remained, crashing waves in and out, in and out. And after a while, it was no longer the ocean but her breath, in and out, in and out.

Rachel opened her eyes. A featureless ceiling was above her, with bright white lights shining from her left and right. She knew where she was at once. She'd been in enough hospitals during the course of her life to know. She sensed motion somewhere in the room so she did her best to sit up, realizing that she was in a bed.

There was a doctor and nurse with one of those rolling computer desks. They were conferring with one another as the doctor took notice of her moving.

"There we are," he said with a smile. He was a middle-aged man with a kind face and the sort of salt-and-pepper hair that looked either very handsome or very messy. On him, it was handsome. "Agent Gift, how are you feeling?"

"Don't know yet," she said. "Groggy. How long have I been here?"

He checked his watch and said, "A little less than two hours. Your partner rushed you over. He's out in the waiting room right now. It seems you got a little overexcited and, according to your records, that is not something you should be doing in your state."

The fact that another doctor knew about her condition alarmed her. Would Anderson find out? Would this go on a report somewhere? She then thought of Jack and wondered if he'd already made the call to Anderson. And had he called Grandma Tate?

"You look concerned," the doctor said. "Let me see if I can ease your mind. We've got some blood tests being run right now just to make sure, but I don't see any serious harm. I'm quite sure you're here from a mixture of things: stress, mild dehydration, and, of course, simple exacerbation from your condition. When you fell, your head even managed to hit the cushion of the passenger seat according to your partner, so there are no bumps or bruises."

"I see." She looked to her arm and saw an IV, likely taking care of the mild dehydration issue. She searched around internally for the slight pain she'd felt in her head just before passing out but it wasn't there. "Could I speak to Jack?"

"Jack? Oh, your partner. Yes, I don't see why not." Before heading out, though, the doctor lingered by her bedside. He seemed to think about something for a moment or two and then sat on the edge of her bed.

"I'm sure you already know this, and it goes without saying, but given your condition, I don't know that it's wise of you continue to work. With some occupations, I'd stay quiet on the matter but as you're an FBI agent with an unpredictable tumor in your brain, I think some smarter decisions need to be made."

"Yes, I know." She did her best not to be snippy or short with him, but that's how she felt. She also felt embarrassed and weak, and she wasn't looking forward to hearing what Jack might have to say when he came into the room.

The doctor simply nodded and then, on his way out, waved the nurse at the mobile station to follow along with him. In the room alone, Rachel let out a soft curse under her breath. Not only was she embarrassed, but she was also once again having to face the fact that she could very well be impeding the progress of the case rather than helping. It made her think of what life might be like a few months down the road when things got worse. Of course, work would be well behind her by then, but what other ways would she be hindering people? To what extent were people like Jack and Grandma Tate supposed to wait on her despite the fact that she'd been so damned stubborn at the start of it all?

"What's wrong with me?" she asked the empty room.

She felt the sting of tears coming on but used a great deal of her energy to fight them off. She thought of Paige at home with Grandma Tate, both of them assuming she was just out and about on a case. She didn't know if she'd tell Grandma Tate about this little incident and could only hope that Jack hadn't taken it upon himself to do it for her. And then, knowing that she was not only choosing the case over Paige but now also keeping more and more things from her, Rachel felt a deep and intense hurt.

"What's wrong with me?" she said again, this time allowing one of those tears to spill down her face. She knew that things may have played out very differently if she hadn't passed out. If *that* hadn't happened, she'd probably be home right now. This fact seemed to dig the knife in deeper, twisting and tearing.

Jack came into the room several minutes later. He was carrying his phone in his hand and a look of sad defeat on his face.

"Sorry about this," she said.

Jack only nodded as he sat down in the single visitor's chair directly beside her bed. "I need to be honest with you, Rachel."

"Okay…"

"You *should* be sorry. Yes, I know I asked you to come along with me on this despite knowing about the tumor and the leave of absence. That's on me. But did I or did I not tell you earlier in the day that I thought it was a bad idea?"

"You did."

"And now I find myself in a situation where I'm going to have to lie to Anderson. There will be paperwork and a record of this visit. We're going to have to keep it from him, which means any report I write up for the case is going to have to omit this. And if that somehow comes back on me in the future, it could be very bad. You understand all of this, right?"

For a moment, she felt very small. He was talking to her in the same way he'd spoken to Wes Dalton in the hotel room.

"All I can do is apologize," she said. "Between the two of us, there was a moment today where I felt incredible. I remember thinking that I hadn't felt so good since getting the news about the tumor. This thing…it came out of nowhere. And honestly, it didn't even hurt all that much. I just got dizzy and sort of…*spinny*. And then I was out."

"The doctors say you're okay from what they can tell. Just waiting on the results of some blood tests, from what I understand."

"That's what I'm told. Jack, did you happen to call my grandmother?"

He sighed and said, "No. I thought about it but then I assumed this was not something you'd want her to know about, given the circumstances. And honestly, it's not the sort of drama I want to willingly step into."

There was a knock at the door and when it opened, the same nurse with the rolling station came inside. She pushed it toward Rachel's bed and offered a smile. "Let's get that IV out, what do you say?"

Rachel and Jack remained silent as the nurse worked. The nurse seemed to understand that she had walked in on a tense conversation because she didn't bother with attempting idle chitchat. She did her job, placed a Band-Aid over the injection site, and then made her exit with a polite wave.

"Rachel, you can't keep doing this," Jack said as soon as the nurse closed the door.

"I know. But it's harder to accept than you might think."

"Oh, no, I think I get it. Look…I have no doubt that you love your daughter and would do anything under the sun to make her happy. But I've also seen you at this job for the past six or seven years. I know what it means to you. I know how passionate you are about it. That's why I haven't been strict about refusing to work with you. I can't even imagine how hard it must be for you to feel like this job is being taken away from you. So I think I *do* get why you're hanging on to it so tightly."

"Jack, I promise you I'm not just being selfish and naïve. Everything I've read and everything the doctors have told me indicate that there will come a time during the progress of this thing that I'll *know* when it's time to accept that the end is coming. My body will start to go weak and my mind won't be as sharp. But I swear, Jack, I just haven't felt that yet. And I don't want to..." She stopped long enough to catch her breath, keeping a sob down as everything in her wanted to weep. "I don't want to stop working on these cases until that day comes."

"This is the second time you've blacked out on the job, Rachel. And that's not even counting the little car accident a few weeks back."

"I know," she said, a bit ashamed. "But I think if we can keep working together like this…and if I can convince Anderson that maybe I was a bit too overzealous in my leave of absence request, I think I have at least a few more cases in me. I can feel it coming on now. And I know I have to take better care of myself. I think I can catch it before it happens now."

He surprised her by reaching out and taking her hand in his. "I hope that's true," he said. "But you also have to understand that every time something like this happens, I feel responsible. Because I *know* what's going on with you and by just allowing you to stay on the job, it's like I'm enabling you. On the other hand, it's not my place to tell you what to do and it's certainly not my place to tell Anderson about your health. In other words…my hands are tied."

"I know, and I'm sorry. I just…I need to work some things out and try to get a better grip on this."

"The bureau has some decent therapists on staff," Jack said. "Have you thought about speaking to one of them about it? They can't tell Anderson, either. Doctor-patient confidentiality."

"Oh my God. Can you see me talking to therapist? I'd probably drive them to quit." She smiled at her own comment, but there was something in it that stirred a thought. She looked to Jack and pointed at him. "Hey…there's an idea."

"What? You going to a therapist?"

"No, not me. I'm thinking about these victims. Who else might know they have these conditions and that they're on a wait list? We're talking more than twenty people on a wait list. At least a few of them would probably be seeing a therapist, right?"

"Maybe," he said, but his widening eyes showed that he thought they might very well be on to something. "But getting that information is going to take some form-filling and a decent amount of time."

"It would if we went through normal channels," she said. "But it's a good thing we've got the Life Fulfilled founder and staff physician under our thumb."

CHAPTER TWENTY FOUR

With no clear idea how long it would take for the blood test results to come back, Rachel got to work. Jack decided to leave, not wanting to stay at the hospital for too long. He was already freaking out about Anderson somehow finding out, so, while Rachel started to dig into the therapists lead, he went back out to interview a few of the people still on the waiting list, hoping to learn more about their experiences with the foundation, Dr. Lucas, and any therapists that may have also been suggested by Life Fulfilled.

Before she started trying to compile information, she thought about something Dr. Lucas had said when they'd surprised him at Vicki Freemont's house. He'd been telling them about the patient he'd accidentally killed, the patient who had received triple the amount of morphine that was needed. Dr. Lucas had specifically mentioned conversations he'd had with the patient's therapist about the morality of assisted suicide. It was more than enough to make Rachel think Lucas was comfortable working hand-in-hand with therapists. In other words, he'd likely be a decent place to start.

Rachel started by calling Life Fulfilled to get his number. She couldn't help but wonder if maybe Wes Dalton had called and notified his staff to be as difficult as possible, throwing up obstacles at every turn now that they had confronted him on his non-professional actions. But she found this not to be the case at all; the receptionist she spoke to at Life Fulfilled was more than happy to provide her with the number.

She called Dr. Lucas and when he answered, it seemed as if he was still shaken from their encounter earlier in the day. He sounded worn down, maybe even a little depressed. She supposed being dragged back through his actions in Tennessee had to take it out of him.

"Agent Gift," he said after she'd introduced herself again. "Please don't take this the wrong way, but I was really hoping to not have to speak with you again."

"Well, I promise it's not going to be quite as difficult this time. Dr. Lucas, I need to know what other professional services are sometimes offered at Life Fulfilled. They offer you as a medical evaluation of sorts, and I know they sometimes help with financial assistance. But I'm wondering if there are any therapists they send their clients to."

"Yes, actually. And really, it's not uncommon with people who have been given a diagnosis of the terminal kind. With Life Fulfilled, every client is required to meet with a therapist at least once." As he explained this, Rachel considered her first doctor's visit back when she'd been first diagnosed. One of the many pamphlets she'd been handed was for local therapists who specialized in this area.

"Is that one visit a prerequisite to get on the waiting list?"

"It is."

"Do you have any idea how many therapists Life Fulfilled works with?"

"Three that I know of for sure. But really, that number has come down to two. One of them left the foundation a few weeks ago. From what I understand, she moved to North Carolina and started working with a private practice."

"Do you know why?"

"I don't. But I can deduce it probably came down to money. From what I gather, the therapists that work with Life Fulfilled aren't given much money. They *are* a non-profit after all. Think about it…there's a reason they got me, a retired doctor who had his license revoked, to come on board."

"Have you worked closely with the two remaining therapists?" Rachel asked.

"Closely, no. But I've met them both and they're both quite pleasant. You can tell they are in their profession because they truly care for people."

"Would you happen to have their names and numbers?" As she asked this question, there was a knock on her door. The same nurse came back in, holding a folder. When she saw that Rachel was on the phone, she simply stood just inside the door, waiting.

"I do," Dr. Lucas said, "but it's all saved in my phone. Hold one second, would you?"

"Of course. Thank you." She then looked to the nurse and gave an apologetic frown. "Sorry."

"Oh, no worries." She approached the bed with the folder. Rachel knew the contents inside the folder were her blood test results and for the first time since being diagnosed, she wasn't worried. Aside from passing out, she truly did feel better than she had in weeks. She was already starting to wonder if what had happened after speaking to Anderson had been nothing more than an overwhelming wave of emotion brought on by the fact that Alex Lynch had somehow managed to evade the US Marshals.

"Good news?" Rachel asked. She still had her phone to her ear while Dr. Lucas searched for the names and numbers of the therapists.

"Good news for sure," the nurse said. "All of your tests are showing better-than-expected results. Your hemoglobin count is a bit higher that we usually like to see, but that's just a result of the dehydration, and we fixed that up with the fluid we gave you. In other words, if you're going to insist on remaining active, just make sure you're getting plenty of fluids."

Another voice spoke up, this one male and right in her ear. "Okay, Agent Gift? I've got those numbers."

"Great. Can you give me just one second?"

"Oh sure."

Rachel looked to the test results, latching on to the term the nurse had used. *Better-than-expected results.* She couldn't help but think of Grandma Tate and her miraculous recovery. And while she wasn't so naïve as to think she'd be granted a similar fate, it did make her feel better about her desire to keep working—at least for a few more weeks

But let's focus on this case first, she thought.

"So everything looks good?" Rachel asked.

"Everything looks great," the nurse responded. "Unless you have any other questions, you're free to go, Agent Gift. Just stop by the desk on your way to the elevators to sign a few things."

"Thanks so much," Rachel said, riding a slight wave of euphoria. She eyed the folder as the nurse carried it back out with her and then turned her attention back to her phone, where Dr. Lucas was still waiting on the other line. "Sorry about that. You were saying?"

"I've got the numbers for you," Lucas said. "The first one is Angie Koontz. She's an older lady, nearing sixty or so." He gave her number and as Rachel committed it to memory, she wondered if the number would be enough. She'd still have the obstacle of a therapist being very protective over a patient's information.

"The second one," Lucas went on, "is Stephen Ayer. He's a younger guy and if memory serves, I think he hails from New York." He recited Stephen Ayer's number and when he was done, Rachel found herself scooting to the edge of the bed. Her episode had been minor enough where she'd not even been stripped and placed in a hospital gown. Literally, all she needed to do was check out of this place.

"One more thing, Dr. Lucas. And I understand you're going to have an issue with this, but I can't stress the importance of it enough. Do you have any sort of access to which therapists met with which clients?"

He was silent for a moment but then answered reluctantly. "Yes, actually. While there's a degree of confidentiality even though it's a non-traditional patient-doctor setup, everything in the Life Fulfilled system is streamlined. I have access to the same network everyone else with the foundation has. From a client's listing, I can tell you what their illness is, who their primary physician is, and which therapist they've seen—among other things."

"And do you have access to it right now?"

"Yes. I'm at home, looking at my laptop right now."

"I need to know which therapists the victims saw," Rachel said. "It could turn out to be a huge help in this case."

"You understand I could get in a great deal of trouble for this, right?"

"I do. And *you* understand, hopefully, that the longer it takes me to get this information, the more time for the killer to strike again."

She could hear him sigh on the other line, but it was followed by the faint clicking of laptop keys. "What are the victims' names?"

"Troy Hetfield, Polly Warren, and Benjamin Wells."

"My God…I…I just spoke with Polly last week." She could hear him collecting himself, clearing his throat, taking a deep breath and maybe even biting back a little sob. "Okay…so, I see here that Benjamin Wells met with Angie Koontz. And for Troy and Polly, it looks like…yes, they both met with Stephen Ayer."

"Are these appointments randomly assigned or is there some sort of logistical thought that goes into which therapist should match up with each client?"

"No, nothing that deep. Much of it just comes down to the therapists' schedules."

"Okay. Thank you for your time, Dr. Lucas."

"No problem. Just…if this thing goes down badly, I'd appreciate it if you could keep my name out of this. I'm sure you understand that I really should not have given you this information."

"Yes, I know. And I'll do what I can to make sure your name isn't mentioned."

She ended the call and instantly typed the two numbers she'd been given into her Notes app. She then slipped her shoes back on and left the hospital room without so much as a glance back. As she made her way down to the desk, she checked her watch. It was getting close to five o'clock in the afternoon. Paige would have been home for about an hour now and Grandma Tate would probably blow a gasket if she stayed out until dark (and rightfully so, Rachel reminded herself).

She made the decision then and there to draw a line in the sand. If she was going to make this work-family balance somehow work in whatever time she had left, she was going to have to start making boundaries for herself and sticking to them. The line she drew was that she would look into Stephen Ayer, maybe pay him a visit if at all possible. And after that, she would go home regardless of how things went with Ayer.

She hurried to the desk and signed three different papers while also handing over her insurance card. She didn't realize that it could be a mistake until after the card had been run. It went through the bureau, which was going to create a paper trail. If the visit was for some reason scrutinized later down the line, she'd have some questions to answer.

Eh, maybe I'll be dead by then, she thought with a bit of morbid humor.

With the discharge process done, she took the elevators down to the main floor. As she crossed the lobby and headed for the doors, she realized that she and Jack had missed one very important detail: she had no car. And while she didn't mind calling for an Uber, she thought she had a better idea. She just hoped she wouldn't have to sell Jack too hard on it.

She called Jack as she stepped through the pneumatic doors and into the afternoon sun. The parking lot was bright and warm, a field of sunlight bouncing from windshields. Jack answered on the fourth ring. His voice was hushed and almost sleepy-sounding. Rachel had worked with him long enough to know that this meant he was within earshot of someone else.

"Where are you?" Rachel asked.

"Standing in the hallway of the McCain residence. Malory McCain is currently fourth on the waiting list. We've been talking about the time she spent with one of the therapists working under the Life Fulfilled umbrella."

"Was it Koontz or Ayer?"

Jack laughed, and she could picture him shaking his head. "Seems like you've gotten a lot done from your hospital bed."

"I'm out of it now. I just checked out a few minutes ago. Now…Koontz or Ayer?"

"Stephen Ayer."

"I just spoke with Dr. Lucas, who confirmed that both Polly Warren and Troy Hetfield also met with Ayer. I don't see a smoking gun yet but I think he's definitely worth a visit."

"Same." She couldn't help but wonder if Ayer might be simply taking his job a little too far. It was, after all, his job to make his patients feel as comfortable as possible. What better way to ease their troubles than by ending their life? It seemed like a stretch, but she knew how deranged the human mind could often be.

"How far away are you from the hospital?" she asked.

"Twenty minutes, give or take. Do you have an address for Ayer?"

"No. Maybe you can get it from the McCains."

"Maybe. And if not, I'll call a request in to the bureau. I'll work on that and text it to you when I get it. You okay grabbing an Uber and meeting me at his address?"

"I can. But…you aren't going to try to talk me out of it? You aren't going to suggest I take that Uber straight home?"

"Rachel, I think that's a great idea. But would it do any good?"

"No."

"Exactly, So let me save that breath for trying to get an address for Ayer. I'll text you when I get it."

He ended the call, the line going dead in Rachel's ear. Feeling anxious and idle, she slowly started to pace around the parking lot, finding a little trail off to the western side of the building that wound through a flower garden. She found a little wooden bench by a small brick column and sat down. Looking out to the wildflowers and the wavering butterflies among the garden, she thought back to the last doctor she'd seen.

His name was Dr. Emerson, and Jack had recommended him to her. He'd given her the same news as the other two doctors—that the tumor in her head was in a place that was pretty much a death sentence in terms of surgical solutions. But he *had* offered her a small crumb of hope in the form of an experimental treatment that could shrink the tumor, making it a bit more realistic to surgically remove. She understood very little of it, something to do with her white blood cells and something called CAR T-cell therapy. Emerson told her there was maybe a ten percent chance that it would work. And when you were staring death in the face, ten percent started to sound like pretty good odds.

When she was trying to solve the murders of people with terminal illnesses, ten percent started to sound *very* good.

As she watched a butterfly land on a hyacinth bloom, she began to nod to herself. She'd go back to Emerson when this case was over. She'd tell him she was interested in the treatment and wanted to start as soon as she could. What the hell could it hurt to at least *try*?

She smiled, surprised to find that prospect excited her a bit. She smiled even wider when her phone dinged at her as a text from Jack came through. There was no lead-up, no small talk. Just Stephen Ayer's address.

As she pulled up her Uber app, she got another text from him. Somehow, her smile grew even wider. The text read: **Race ya!**

With a strange revitalization passing through her body, she quickly booked a ride, finding that a car could be there to pick her up within six minutes. She sat on the bench and watched the parking lot, waiting for the car to take her to what she hoped would be a significant break in the case or, at least, a new source of information on their victims.

CHAPTER TWENTY FIVE

When Rachel's Uber pulled alongside the curb in front of Stephen Ayer's house, she saw that Jack had beaten her there. He was sitting in the bureau sedan and gave her a little mocking wave as her car pulled in behind his. Rachel paid her tip with the app and then quickly got into the sedan's passenger seat.

"Slowpoke," he said. "I've been here for like five minutes."

"Easy for you to say. You stranded me at the hospital."

"Speaking of which, you got out of there pretty quickly. I take it the blood tests came back fine?"

"They did. And blackout aside, I do feel good. *Really* good. It makes me wonder what they *really* put in that IV."

"Oh, that," he said, opening the door with a smile. "I told that nurse to make sure to put some tequila in it."

As they made their way up the sidewalk to Stephen Ayer's two-story brick home, it occurred to her just how much like a machine she and Jack often seemed. Most partners played off of one another; that is, if one was in a sour mood, the other served as a balance of sorts and tried to remain in a positive mood. But for her and Jack, it was the opposite. When one was in a bad mood, the other felt it and sympathized and usually shared the same mood. But in an instant like right now, her good mood and energetic feeling was reflected in him. There were times when she felt that they were best friends who just happened to have the same career and had been partnered together. Now was one of those times, and it was exactly what she needed in the face of her current ordeals.

She did, however, have to remind herself that she was on leave when they stepped up onto the porch. Jack knocked the large, brass handle in the center of the door. A dog started barking delightedly inside, the sound of its nails on a hardwood floor quite clear through the door.

A male voice accompanied the dog, speaking to it in dulcet tones. The man's voice drew closer and the door opened up for them. A glass door sat on the other side, and a handsome middle-aged man stood there. He seemed to be dressed in work clothes—a button-down baby blue shirt, a black tie, and slacks. Rachel wondered if he'd just gotten home from work.

"Yes?" he asked. "Can I help you?"

Jack showed his ID, holding it up close to the glass. "We're Agents Rivers and Gift, with the FBI. Are you Dr. Stephen Ayer?"

"I am," the man said, tilting his head curiously as he looked at the ID.

"Could we come in, sir?" Jack asked.

He was still clearly confused, but he nodded and said, "Sure, sure. Is everything okay?"

As he opened the door, Rachel noticed the gorgeous Labrador sitting obediently by the edge of the door. Ayer had to keep his hand on the dog's collar as they entered the house. The dog wagged its tail as it watched their guests come inside.

"We aren't sure, actually," Jack said, answering Ayer's question. "We'd like to ask you some questions about your work with Life Fulfilled."

"Is that right?" Ayer asked, still confused. Rachel didn't think he looked concerned, but simply baffled. Maybe they *had* just caught him coming in from work and he was trying to process this sudden and unexpected visit from the Federal Bureau of Investigation.

"Is that where you were working today?" Rachel asked. "It seems we may be catching you just as you've gotten home."

"Pretty close, actually. I've been home for about twenty minutes or so." He led them through his foyer and into the adjoining living room. The floors here were also hardwood and the place had a minimalist feel to it. Both the couch and the armchair were very small yet efficient and the television, mounted on the wall, almost looked as if it had been birthed out of the house itself. Everything was smooth and unblemished, no clutter or mess anywhere. The walls were a creamy eggshell white and only a single thing hung from the wall—an abstract painting of what Rachel thought might be a strange oceanscape.

Ayer gestured to the couch. "Sit down, please. And to answer your question, no, I did not work with Life Fulfilled today."

"How often would you say you work with them?" Rachel asked.

"Once a week. Maybe as little as once every two weeks, depending on my schedule. Why…is there something going on?"

"Dr. Ayer," Jack said, "do you recall the names Polly Warren and Troy Hetfield?"

"Yes. I met with Troy earlier this week. Polly…I suppose it was about three weeks ago? Maybe as much as a month."

"How many times did you meet with them?" Jack asked.

"Just once each time. But I tell you...I would love to have Troy as a permanent client. There's something about him...so uplifting and happy, even in the face of his terrible diagnosis." He clasped his hands together and looked cautiously at the agents. "I'm sorry, but what is this about?"

"Dr. Ayer," Jack said, "both Troy and Polly are dead. They've been murdered within the past week."

Ayer looked as if he'd been punched in the stomach. It was hard to tell against the white walls, but he looked as if he'd gone slightly pale. "Oh my God. Are you...I mean, I just spoke with Troy. He was..."

"There has been a third as well," Rachel said, "but he was seen by Dr. Koontz."

It seemed to take a few seconds, but Ayer seemed to finally understand what they were implying. "You mean...is someone hunting down Life Fulfilled clients?"

"It appears that way," Rachel said. "People on the waiting list."

"And here's the hard part," Jack said. "If someone is actively seeking out people on the Life Fulfilled waiting list, it means that the killer has the list. And we're assuming it's not the sort of thing Mr. Dalton or anyone else with the foundation would just willingly give to people. So we can't help but wonder if the killer is someone on the inside. And seeing as how you spoke to two of the three victims, you have to be considered."

This time, it looked like he'd been slapped hard across the face. "Me? Are you insane?"

As they let him continue to accept what was being presented to him, Rachel watched the Lab prance by the entrance to the room. He looked inside, checked out his guests, and then walked elsewhere, just out of sight. She could hear him sniffing at something, his nails still clicking against the floors.

"You have to understand where we're coming from," Jack went on. "If the killer is using the list, that at least means we have a group of people we know need to be watched after and protected. But on the flip side of that, we also have to assume the killer would have easy access to the list. Now, you're not the first person we've questioned about it, Dr. Ayer. And if you can provide alibis for where you have been over the past several days, we can eliminate you from the equation."

"This is...this is just..."

Ayer couldn't find the words to express himself, and the hell of it was that Rachel didn't think he even appeared all that angry. If anything, he seemed wrecked that two people he'd recently met with had been murdered.

"I know it's a lot," Rachel said. "So, just think it over. Calm down and just replay your last few days."

It wasn't until she said this that she realized she was convinced he wasn't the killer. It all came down to the way he'd reacted upon hearing the news. He continued to look back and forth between them, almost as if he was expecting them to reveal that this was all some sort of sick joke.

"Well, let's see…this week," he said. "Monday, I was at the office from eight in the morning until four in the afternoon. After that, I came home and…"

He was shaking a bit and still finding it hard to express himself. He got up from the couch and shook his head. "I'm sorry. I just need to think…to let this sink in. I think I need a drink. Can I offer you anything?"

"No, thank you," Jack said.

Rachel nearly said the same, but remembered the nurse and the doctor back at the hospital, telling her how part of the cause of her blackout was dehydration. "You know, if it's not too much trouble, I think I'll have a glass of water."

"Of course," Ayer said. He walked back out into the hallway and toward a large kitchen that sat slightly off-center of the hallway's end. Though he did not invite them to join him, Jack and Rachel followed along. As they made their way, she saw the Lab again, standing by a closed door along the hallway. He grinned up at them, tail wagging again. Rachel leaned down and stroked him between the ears. The dog's tail wagged harder, but Rachel only gave him a few seconds of her attention, forging on into the kitchen.

When Ayer had said he needed a drink, he'd been talking about liquor. He was reaching up into a cabinet by a stainless-steel fridge and taking down a bottle of scotch. When he then took a tumbler out of a nearby cabinet he also took out a glass. He handed it to Rachel and said, "Help yourself," while nodding to the water dispenser built into the door of the refrigerator.

He poured himself a nice amount of scotch and took a long gulp. For a moment, Rachel though he was going to knock it all back at once but he restrained himself. He took a very deep breath and then tried to start talking again. Rachel sipped on her water as patiently as she could.

"Okay…my schedule for the last week. I was at work, with the practice I work for, on Monday from eight to four. I left there and came home. I was…no, wait, I went to the grocery store first. Got home maybe a little after five. Tuesday, I worked half a day and spoke with Troy Hetfield at the Life Fulfilled offices. The rest of the week, I was at my own office, working. I've got schedules and case notes you can see to back it all up."

"That should be enough," Rachel said. "The only missing piece would be the fact that Troy Hetfield was killed at night, in a parking lot after a concert, just last night. Where were you last night?"

"Here. From about six o'clock on. I sat here with Rascal—my dog—and watched TV. Messed around with my guitar for a little while," he said quickly as if ashamed.

"Any online activity we can look into to back that up?" Jack asked.

The tight look on Ayer's face was clear sign that he was very frustrated that they would even think he'd be capable of murder. But he was also trying to be as calm and as polite as possible. It was yet another thing that made Rachel quite certain that he was not their killer.

"I checked my work emails around eight or so," he said. "I looked up some guitar tabs at some point. Maybe around nine thirty? Not sure…and that was on my phone, so…"

"Do you live alone, Dr. Ayer?" Rachel asked.

"Yes. I have a girlfriend that stays over sometimes, but she's been overseas for the past two weeks. Oh! Yes! I also spoke to her on my phone last night. Just before bed…right around eleven."

"That could help," Jack said. "If it comes down to it, you'd be willing to let us look at your phone records?"

"Absolutely!"

"That's good, Dr. Ayer. I think for now, we'll leave you alone but just know that until your alibis have all checked out or we can prove your innocence otherwise, we may have police cars passing by your home here and there. And we may also contact you with more questions."

"Yes, of course. Anything I can do to help."

Rachel and Jack shared a look of agreement, a non-verbal exchange solidifying that their conversation with Stephen Ayer was over—and that he was almost certainly not their killer.

Rachel finished her water and gave Ayer a thankful smile. "Thank you for your time," she said.

"Sure, of course."

Ayer followed them out of the kitchen, shadowing them as they made their way back down the hallway. Once again, Rachel stopped to give the Lab—Rascal—some attention. This time, the dog came to her and looked up for the attention, his tongue lolling as Rachel stroked him on the head and under the neck.

"He's a gorgeous dog," Rachel commented. "How old?"

"Five years now," Ayer said, his voice still shaky. "And spoiled rotten."

Rachel gave Rascal's head one final rub and as she looked away, her eyes once again went to the door Rascal had been standing in front of the entire time. She recalled that Rascal had been sniffing around it curiously when they arrived. Even this little detail may have meant nothing to Rachel…but then she saw the two small scratches along the doorframe, exactly where the door met flush with the wood.

And just below those marks on the door, a section of the door that looked as if it had recently been washed or polished in some way—but just that one small section. The door itself was a soft chestnut brown in color but a small space roughly the size of a playing card stood out much more than the rest of it, brighter and almost shining.

"What's in this room?" Rachel asked, nodding to the door as Rascal licked at her hand, wanting some more love.

"The basement," Ayer answered. "Mainly just storage. It's unfinished…one of those things I said I'd eventually get done and turn it into a gym."

There was just the tiniest bit of theatrics to the explanation. Not in the words themselves, but how he delivered them. He'd spoken quite fast when he'd tried to recall the events of his past week but here, he seemed to be passing off the explanation of the basement as if he was no longer overly concerned about being under suspicion of murder. It was in his tone, which had suddenly become almost warm and friendly. It was an *incredibly* small detail, but Rachel picked up on it.

"Can we have a look?" Rachel asked.

Once more, Ayer went pale. He stepped forward quickly and then seemed to realize what he had done. Any hope of remaining cool and collected was demolished in that moment and it became clear that Stephen Ayer did *not* want them to go down into his basement. And with that realization, the two scratch marks at the edge of the doorframe and the spot that had obviously been scrubbed recently seemed much more sinister.

"Stay where you are, Dr. Ayer," Jack said. He took a moment to size up the situation, looking at Rachel. Again, she understood that her temporary leave of absence was getting in the way. She didn't have a gun so any splitting up was going to be tricky.

"What's down there, Dr. Ayer?" she asked.

"N-nothing." He was near tears now and his body seemed to have locked up.

Jack reached out and placed his hand on Ayer's shoulder. "Step back into the living room, Dr. Ayer," he said. When Ayer still didn't move, Jack gave him a light push. "Now, sir, or I *will* draw my weapon."

The slight rise in Jack's voice made Ayer cringe. He let out a little gasp as he finally started to walk back to the living room, weeping. Rascal followed, not sure what was happening to his master.

"You go down," Jack said. "Any sign of danger, you haul ass back up here." Then, with a tight frown on his face, he withdrew his Glock and handed it over to her. Rachel knew that taking it was risky; if she had to fire it, she and Jack would have to come up with an extravagant lie to keep her clear of the house and, by default, his gun and the case.

She shook her head, realizing the implications of it all. "No," she said. "Keep it. I'll be fine."

Jack nodded and holstered it, but it was apparent that he didn't like it. He looked back to Ayer and said, "Last chance."

But Ayer was struggling with some sort of emotional trauma that wouldn't allow him to speak. Whatever was waiting for them downstairs was going to potentially wreck his life. And with that in mind, Rachel approached the door, turned the knob, and opened the door.

CHAPTER TWENTY SIX

The staircase was made of unfinished wood—the first indication that at least one thing Ayer had told them was correct. The basement was indeed unfinished. There was a single light switch on the door going down to the bottom of the stairs. She flipped it on and could see a concrete floor at the bottom. As she made her way down, she could hear Rascal back at the door, sniffing.

At the bottom of the stairs, she could see where the builders had put down the rudimentary framing of the basement. If Ayer ever wanted to actually finish it, he had the guidelines to go by. There was a single, large room to the back of the basement that had been walled off with nothing more than sheetrock. To her right, there was the wooden framing of a smaller room; the plumbing guides and two pipes coming out of the wall suggested it was supposed to be a bathroom. There was more framing immediately to the left as she came to the end of the stairs. She could see pencil markings along the boards, mostly arrows and numbers left by the builders.

The basement was eerily quiet and easily ten degrees cooler than it had been upstairs. Before advancing forward, Rachel took a moment to study the floor and the sheetrock frame of the one walled-off room. She saw nothing at first, but as she finally took a step forward she did see a slight flaw in the concrete floor.

Or, rather, not a flaw but a smear. It was similar to the cleaned space she'd seen on the door upstairs. Something on the floor had been wiped up. She could now see two places, making an arced path over to the doorway of the room that had been sheetrocked over. Her hand reached down for a gun that wasn't there and at the same time, she heard a slight commotion from upstairs. There were a series of footsteps, the sound of a slight struggle, and then a loud thumping noise. A few seconds passed and she could then hear a soft mewling noise, like someone beginning to weep. She imagined that Ayer had tried to get up and make a run for it, or to attack Jack. If that were indeed the case, the loud thump was no doubt Ayer hitting the floor. Jack might very well be cuffing him in that very moment.

And if Ayer *had* taken such a measure, it made her very uneasy about what might be waiting for her in the room in front of her. She walked a bit faster to the room, not wanting to make Jack wait any longer.

The light switch she'd hit on the way down the stairs had not affected the room. It was dark inside, like walking toward the mouth of a cave. When she finally walked through what was intended to one day be a doorway, she found another light switch. This one had simply been installed; there was no cover over it, showing the wiring behind it, snaking up the boards within the wall. She tried it anyway and found that a light did indeed come on—an overhead bulb without a cover.

And when her eyes fell on what waited for her, Rachel flinched and let out a curse under her breath.

A woman lay on a pile of blankets. She was quite pretty—blonde, and maybe twenty-five years of age, dressed in a crop-top and jeans. She was lying on her back and looking up to the unfinished ceiling. She did not move or flinch at all when Rachel turned on the light. And though this told Rachel everything she needed to know, she still couldn't help but to call out.

"Hey," she said. "Ma'am, are you…"

She was dead. It became even more apparent the closer Rachel got to her. The basement seemed to go colder as the realization sunk in. The excitement of the potential huge leads dissolved into sadness as Rachel knelt by the pile of blankets and placed her fingers to the woman's neck. The skin was cold and there was no pulse. She saw that there was a bandage on the other side of the woman's neck, made up of hastily applied gauze and multiple layers of athletic tape. Little splotches of blood had come through, staining the gauze. That, she supposed, answered what the little cleaned areas on the floor and the door had been. She'd bled on those surfaces and Ayer had done his best to clean it up.

As for the scratches in the doorframe upstairs, those were likely the result of a struggle. Two fingernails on the woman's right hand were bent backwards, one pulled nearly completely out of the finger.

Rachel stood up and looked down at the body. There wasn't much discoloration and there was no noticeable odor. Also, the blood stains on the gauze were still rather bright. If she had to guess, this woman had not been dead for any more than three days.

She slowly backed away and headed for the stairs. She wondered which member of the waiting list was currently dead in Dr. Ayer's basement, which name they could now cross off. Angry, she hurried up the stairs. She opened the door to the hallway so quickly that she nearly slammed it into Rascal, still waiting at the door.

"Who is she, Dr. Ayer?" Rachel asked even before she made it into the living room. When she got there, she saw that her assumption had been correct. Ayer was lying on his chest on the floor, his arms pulled behind him with his wrists cuffed. Jack stood next to him, hands on his hips as Rachel entered the room.

"Who is she?" Rachel asked again, her voice bitter and thin.

Ayer only moaned in agony, as if he'd been the one who was injured and deposited in a basement.

"What am I missing?" Jack asked.

"There's a dead woman in his basement. Looks to be recent."

"I didn't mean to," Ayer whined. "I thought she was happy, and she just…she changed her mind and I couldn't. I couldn't…"

He started to hyperventilate on the floor. Jack reached down and helped him to his feet, repositioning him and placing him on the couch.

"Is she also on the waiting list?" Jack asked him.

But Ayer had no intention of talking. He was too busy weeping and shaking his head. The only thing he managed to get out was "I didn't mean it. I didn't mean it."

As Ayer broke down on the couch, Jack stepped closer over to Rachel. "Can you stay here with him for a second? I can't let it get out that you were here. Let me check the scene out and I'll come back up. But I need you to leave, Rachel. You understand that, right?"

She did understand it. It was what was best for both of them in that moment but damn, did it hurt. While she badly wanted to be with Paige, her leaving after such a discovery almost felt like giving up.

"I'll call for another Uber," she said.

"Okay. Are you good with him?"

She observed Ayer on the couch, still losing himself in a tide of emotion that seemed to be tearing him apart on the inside.

"Yeah, I'm fine. Just go."

He nodded and rushed over to the hallway as Rascal came into the living room and started sniffing at Ayer. And as Ayer continued to wail and try to get control over himself, Rachel ordered another ride on her app, wondering just how difficult it was going to be to wrap this part of the case without getting either her or Jack into a world of trouble.

CHAPTER TWENTY SEVEN

It was 6:33 p.m. when Rachel arrived home. After the car pulled away, she stood on the sidewalk for a moment, looking at her house. The living room curtains were open and she could see Grandma Tate moving around. Rachel had no idea how the tension between them would play out. As a matter of fact, with the exception of the phone call they'd had earlier in the day, Rachel couldn't recall any time she and her grandmother had exchanged cross words.

She knew that she was going to have to work hard to make sure she was completely present this evening. She needed to show Paige that she really was trying to make her a priority and to show Grandma Tate that her career wasn't as important as her family. It would be difficult because her mind already wanted to pull in the direction of Stephen Ayer. She wished she could be there in the interrogation room to hear all of the details—to know what the hell was happening with Jack and all that he was learning from the man. After what she'd found down in his basement, it was borderline torture for her to have to come home and put on the domestic mask.

But her daughter was worth it. And as long as she could keep Paige's face front and center in her mind, she'd be fine. It was usually even easier when she was actually *with* Paige, spending time with her, seeing her smile and listening to her stories that just seemed to go on and on.

Rachel slowly made her way to the front door. Just before she reached it, she received a text message from Jack. She read it twice because it wasn't at all what she'd been expecting. And it put an entirely new spin on the case.

Ayer's victim is a woman named Becka Follin. Not on the LF waiting list but was reported missing in Lynchburg four months ago. Will call with details when interrogation is over.

It was a bit of a bombshell and while it connected Ayer to a different crime, she knew it didn't automatically rule him out as their killer. But even then, as she opened the front door, she felt Ayer slipping away. She knew that the sort of mind that dwelled on things like kidnapping could sometimes be completely different from a mind that fixated on murder—especially the type of mind that fixated on murdering people with recently diagnosed terminal illnesses.

What a mess, she thought.

As she closed the door behind her, Rachel smelled what she thought was pepperoni. And as she crossed the living room into the kitchen, she saw that she was right. Grandma Tate and Paige were sitting at the kitchen table with a large pizza between them. When Paige turned and saw her mother headed her way, she jumped out of her seat and came running over. They hugged right between the living room and kitchen, Paige planting a big, wet kiss on her cheek.

"You came home!" Paige said.

"Well, of course I came home, silly."

"Yeah, but Grandma said she wasn't sure when you'd be home. She said I might be asleep when you got home."

"Well, here I am! Did you save me any pizza?"

"Yeah. We got the extra large because Grandma wanted you to have something to eat when you got home."

Rachel looked over at Grandma Tate and, making sure their eyes connected, said, "Well, that was very kind of Grandma, wasn't it?"

She joined them at the table and as she ate a slice of pizza, there was an obvious tension between her and Grandma Tate, but Paige seemed unaware of it. She went on and on, telling them both about her day and then telling them how much she wanted to see the new Disney movie that she'd seen a preview for.

Rachel gave Paige her undivided attention. She did her best to stay in the zone, making sure she didn't miss a word or a smile. Rachel had never decided what she thought happened when people died. A lot of the time, she just assumed it was like a very big sleep and you just never wake up. You don't know you're dead, therefore, you don't miss being alive. But sitting there and looking at how animated and in love with just about everything her daughter seemed to be, she could not imagine death. She could not imagine any state of being (or, rather, not being) where she would not get to see that smile, to not hear those giggles, to not see those bright eyes. It had her thinking of Dr. Emerson's treatments again and it was the first time since receiving her diagnosis that she felt the strong urge to fight her ailment.

They finished dinner, cleaned up, and sat out on the back porch as the sun set, playing Uno. Rachel then marched upstairs with Paige as bedtime came around and snuggled into bed with her.

"Hey, Mommy, can I ask you something?" Paige asked. The room was lit only by her Paw Patrol nightlight and she looked beautiful in the dimness of it.

"Of course you can."

"When you told me about how you were sick, you said you were going to stop working so much. But you haven't. Did you change your mind?"

The question hurt a bit, but she knew she deserved it. And she figured if her daughter was brave enough to ask such a question, she deserved the truth. "No, I haven't changed my mind. But sometimes there are things that happen—really bad things that happen to good people. And with my job, I'm supposed to help those good people. I'm supposed to keep them safe. And yes...I said I would stop working so much. But right now, I really need to help keep some people safe."

"So it's an important case?"

"Yes, it's a very important case."

"How much longer will it take you to catch the bad people?"

"I don't know, baby. Hopefully not too long."

"And what about after that? Ae you still going to work?"

"I just don't know, sweetie. We'll see. But even if I do work for a bit longer, I'm going to do my best to make sure I'm here more than I have been in the past. Okay?"

Paige nodded, but her expression showed that she either didn't fully understand the answer or understood it perfectly fine but didn't like it.

"What is it? What's wrong?"

"I'm scared about you dying, Mommy." She wasn't crying yet, but her little eyes were glistening with tears. "Daddy left and soon you won't be here. And it scares me. I want you to keep catching the bad people and keeping good people safe but I want you here, too. I...it makes me feel selfish."

She hugged her close, mainly so Paige wouldn't see her cry. "You're not being selfish. It's a very confusing time, I know," she said, trying to keep her voice steady. "I don't know what work will look like after this important case. How do you want ti to look?"

"I know you like your job, and it's a cool job," she said, wiping a tear away. "I want you to keep people safe. And I think you should. I just..I miss you more now that I know...I know about you being sick. I miss daddy, too."

"And we're going to keep letting you and Daddy see each other. He knows it's just going to be you and him when I'm gone...and even though he's not here right now, he loves you very much. And I'm going to try some things…some things at the doctor. It's a very small chance, but I could maybe be around longer than we thought."

"Maybe forever?" Paige asked hopefully.

Rachel hugged Paige tighter and said, "Not forever. But *some time*."

Paige had nothing left to say. She fell quiet and fell asleep roughly five minutes later, still in Rachel's arms. Rachel remained there for several more minutes, just enjoying the feel of her daughter in her arms. It was far too easy to remember her as a baby, fitting right in the crook of her arm and looking up at her with all the love and hope in the world, having no idea just how unfair the world could be at times.

When Rachel finally left the bedroom, she was in tears. She took some time to collect herself in the upstairs bathroom before returning downstairs. She found Grandma Tate sitting on the couch, playing with a jigsaw puzzle app on her iPad. The moment Rachel sat down next to her, she put the iPad down and looked over at her.

"How are you, Rachel?"

For a very brief moment, Rachel almost decided to tell her about her blackout and ensuing trip to the hospital. And though she didn't like the idea of being dishonest in this situation, she also didn't see the point in making the coming conversation more dramatic than it needed to be.

"I'm okay. Clear-headed and pain free for the last few days. I daresay I feel almost normal."

Grandma Tate looked down to her hands for a second, deep in thought. A frown touched the corners of her mouth and she started rubbing her hands together.

"No need to be nervous," Rachel said. "Just say what you feel you need to say."

"I'm just curious about this case you're on. Because I know that you would never flippantly go back on something you told Paige. Despite how I may have come across on the phone today, I know deep down that you would never do anything to hurt her. So it makes me assume that whatever this case is, it has its hooks in you in a way that I could never possibly understand."

Rachel was glad to take the conversation anywhere other than her hospital visit. More than that, she also knew that she needed to vocalize the case. Working it out verbally with Jack was one thing, but actually processing it with someone who didn't know the ins and outs of how the FBI worked might do her some good.

"Someone is killing people who have recently been diagnosed with terminal illnesses. It's…well, it's hitting me harder than I expected."

"Oh my goodness," Grandma Tate said, her hand going to her heart. "That's awful. And yes, I can see how that would upset you. I don't even know how you can manage to work on it. Doesn't it seem personal?"

"I know better than to see it like that," Rachel explained. "But yes, it sort of does feel personal. And I think that's why it's wrapped me up as much as it did."

"So did you get some sort of break? Is that how you were able to come home?"

"Well, I'm not supposed to officially be on the case because of my two-week leave of absence—a leave that I requested and wasn't handed down to me from above for disciplinary actions. So I've really just been helping Jack. We have a suspect right now. Jack is interrogating him. I'm hoping it'll pay off, but…"

"You don't think it's the right person?" Grandma Tate asked.

"I'm just not sure. It doesn't quite feel right."

"That little girl upstairs needs you," Grandma Tate said, switching the subject with an eerie sort of ease that Rachel was convinced only the elderly possess. "But she loves you so much that she's not going to question any decision you make. You understand that, right?"

"I do. And I'm trying, Grandma. I just…I think work has been so important to me for so long that it's harder than I thought to walk away from it. Especially in the midst of cases like this one. But I *have* decided that I'm going to go back to see Dr. Emerson—the doctor Jack recommended that thinks he can use a white blood cell–oriented approach. It's only a ten percent chance but I have to try. Not for me or for my job, but for Paige."

Grandma Tate smiled and reached over to take Rachel's hand. "That's wonderful, Rachel. Any hope is better than none. And if you need a miracle story, look no farther than the old woman sitting in front of you."

"Well, I already told Paige I'll be trying, so there's no backing out now. I think it's best to—"

She was interrupted by the ringing of her phone. When she saw Jack's name on the display, she gave Grandma Tate with an apologetic look. "I'm sorry. It's Jack. He was going to call after they knew more from the interrogation."

"Then answer it," she said, getting to her feet. "I'll go make some tea."

Rachel answered the call as Grandma Tate got up and headed into the kitchen. "Jack, how's it going?"

"It's going a bit odd, to tell you the truth," Jack said. He sounded both tired and wired, a confusing indicator of how the interrogation might have gone.

"I'd expect nothing less," she said.

"Well, for starters, there was a lot more crying once we got him into a room. And I mean, he *broke*. I thought we were going to have to send someone in there to sedate him. So, like I already told you in the text, the dead woman in his basement was a woman named Becka Follin—twenty years old, went missing about four months ago in Lynchburg. And from the small bit we currently know about her, she was perfectly healthy. No terminal illness at all. Once Ayer came around, he told us everything. So now it's just a matter of checking up on his story to make sure it's true. And already, we've got a few boxes checked."

"So what was his story?"

"He was in Lynchburg for a week, helping out with an intensive class at a university up there. He claims to have run into Becka at a bar he stopped by after class one day. Becka was a student at the college he was visiting, though not a psych student, so she wouldn't have been in his class. He says they hit it off, had too much to drink, and ended up back at his hotel room. He claims they were really into one another and she came by every single night until he had to leave. On that last night, he asked her to come to Richmond with him and she got spooked. Came out and called him crazy and obsessive. He said things got out of hand and he admits to threatening her. He'd taught his last class that day and just straight up kidnapped her. He told her he had a gun in his suitcase, which he didn't. He pushed her around a bit, a few punches and slaps, and he took her home with him, all the way to Richmond. She's been in his basement every day since. He says he had physical relations with her a few times and that he thought it was perfectly fine since she'd been more than happy to sleep with him before. But he said for the most part, he just tried talking to her."

"Then how did she die?"

"He says he poisoned her. Put something in a Coke he brought down for her. Some chemical I can't even pronounce. We sent it to the coroner so they can confirm. We also confirmed that he was indeed a participating guest lecturer at the college and that Becka Follin was indeed a senior at the college."

"Does he have alibis for the three murders we're looking into?"

"No. He says he finds it sadly ironic that Becka is the one person that could confirm he was at home but she, of course, is just as dead as our victims."

"Did he mention anything at all about working as a therapist for Life Fulfilled?" Rachel asked.

"Yeah, and gave us the names of everyone he's worked with while under the Life Fulfilled umbrella. He's not denying that he had access to the victims and their issues, but he is adamantly saying he didn't kill then. And you know…I mean, if he's so openly fessing up about Becka Follin, I just don't know why he'd be so sternly arguing against killing these other three."

"What's the consensus with Anderson and everyone else involved?"

"There's a vibe that this might be it—that Ayer might be our guy. I'm on the way over to his house with a small crew to tear the place apart, looking for any clues. But just based on the way he was acting in that interrogation room, I don't think it's him."

"Why not?"

"Because when he was telling me all about Follin, he looked almost relieved. It was like he *needed* to get it all off of his chest. Once it started coming, it just wouldn't stop. He even tried going into detail about their sexual escapades while he was in Lynchburg."

"Where is he now?"

"He's currently in a holding cell. He's been set up for a psychiatric evaluation in the morning and we've got him on suicide watch. In other words, Rachel, he's not going anywhere, and even if there are breaks in this case overnight, nothing is going to move until tomorrow. So you stay home and get it out of your head."

"I will. But if you find anything at his house, will you text me?"

"Absolutely."

"Thanks for the update, Jack."

"Yeah, no problem. Everything good at home?"

She looked into the kitchen, where Grandma Tate was pouring water from the kettle into two cups with waiting tea bags. "Yeah, I think they are. I actually think things are better than I expected here."

"Good. Well, one way or another, I'll talk to you tomorrow."

"Sounds good. Good night, Jack."

She ended the call and thought about what tomorrow might bring. It was rare that both she and Jack were ever both in complete agreement that a suspect who seemed to be guilty was not the right man. It made her think hard about what the day would bring tomorrow if Ayer was somehow proven totally innocent.

Would she be able to sit idly by, taking another back seat or even remaining here at home while Jack was out there looking for the killer?

She wasn't sure. But the fact that Becka Follin had not been terminally ill (from what they knew) made her quite sure that Stephen Ayer was not the killer they were looking for. It did, however, make her really wonder about what the hell sort of circus Life Fulfilled was truly putting on. They had a retired doctor who had been stripped of his license, a CEO who was sleeping with a terminally ill woman who had come to them for help, and a part-time therapist who had kidnapped and killed a woman. There seemed to be a rotten core within the foundation, which made her almost certain that their killer was someone on the inside. And given her own current situation, she thought she might be able to figure it out rather easily—and she could do it without a badge or gun.

"Here you are," Grandma Tate said, setting a cup of peppermint tea down in front of her. She settled down on the couch where she'd been before and started sipping from her own cup. "Everything okay with Jack and his interrogation?"

"We're not sure just yet," Rachel said, still thinking about her fairly simple plan. "But I think I'll have all the answers I need tomorrow."

<h1 style="text-align:center">CHAPTER TWENTY EIGHT</h1>

Rachel woke up the following morning and decided to play things out as normally as possible. The first thing she did when she stirred awake at 6:10 was check her texts and emails. She saw that Jack had indeed texted her around one in the morning. And, as she expected, there was nothing in Stephen Ayer's house to suggest that he had been killing terminally ill patients who had been seeking help from Life Fulfilled.

The text read: **Found some questionable emails from female patients and a few memberships to fetish porn sites. Becka's prints on the doorframe to the basement and her hairs all over the place but nothing to link Ayer to our case. Will touch base tomorrow.**

Realizing that their case was very much still open, Rachel placed her plan firmly aside as she went downstairs. She put coffee on and started making a breakfast of pancakes and eggs. As the first batch of pancakes stiffened on the griddle, Grandma Tate joined her in the kitchen, with Paige coming down ten minutes later.

"You haven't cooked breakfast in *forever*," Paige said as she delightedly poured syrup on her pancakes.

"I wouldn't say *forever*," Rachel said. "But yeah…it's been a while. And if it's okay with Grandma Tate, I think I'd like to take you to school this morning, too."

"Oh, yay!" she said, shoveling syrup-soaked pancake into her mouth.

"Now, you make sure you get some eggs, too," Rachel said. "Eat up. I'm going to drag Grandma Tate into the living room for a second, okay? Don't choke on those pancakes. Chew. Don't swallow them whole."

Paige giggled, a little trickle of syrup running down her chin. Rachel stood up from the table with her coffee in hand and waved Grandma Tate to follow her. Rachel didn't bother sitting, as she didn't expect to spend much time going over what she had on her mind. She glanced back into the kitchen to make sure Paige wasn't trying to eavesdrop before starting.

"I wanted to run this by you," Rachel said, "because I think you deserve to know what's going on. You were right yesterday…on just about everything. I feel like I may be taking you for granted and that's not fair."

"Rachel, all I was—"

"Hold on a second. Let me finish. I just wanted to let you know that I *am* going to head out this morning after I take Paige to school. But I'm not going out with Jack. While it *is* related to the case, it's sort of on an unofficial scale. And unless something drastic comes up, I should be back in plenty of time to be here when Paige gets home."

"I appreciate all of that, Rachel. But really, you don't need to fill me in to that level."

"I think I really do," she said. "You've been an enormous help here ever since Peter left. I don't know how I would have survived it all without your help."

"As long as you try to take care of yourself and are now at least considering going after this thing," she said, softly tapping the side of Rachel's head, "I'm glad to do it. Now, let's get back in there. The little one is trying to listen in, I think."

Rachel nodded and blinked back tears as she went back into the kitchen. She checked her watch and said, "Fifteen minutes, Paige."

"Okay," she said, sliding her last bite of pancake through a little pond of syrup on her plate. "I just have to brush my teeth and I'll be ready."

Rachel sat back down at the table and had her own pancake. She ate and sipped on her coffee and started to think about the best way to go about enacting the small plan she'd been working out in her head since last night.

***

It did Rachel a world of good to realize just how excited Paige was to have her mother taking her to school. After sitting in the drop-off lane for about ten minutes, Rachel received a big hug and a wet kiss on the cheek before Paige got out and headed into the school building. Rachel wondered if every parent had the odd pain of watching their child enter a school—a feeling of pride but also of profound sadness.

It clung to her as she pulled away from the school and headed in the direction of downtown. Before she arrived at her destination, she thought she had a decent idea of how to pull off her plan without getting into any real trouble. And while the news of her tumor may become wider knowledge when she was done, she thought she could

140

probably play it off as a bit of theatrics—something she had to make up in order to get the job done.

She pulled her car along the side of the curb in front of Life Fulfilled at 8:52. The signage on the front door told her that office hours didn't start until nine, so she sat in her car for those eight minutes, putting the pieces together. She supposed that Jack must be feeling an odd sort of victory this morning, if he was awake yet. While she was still convinced that Stephen Ayer wasn't their killer, they'd manage to nab a killer anyway, and that was always a good feeling. She thought about texting him to check in, but didn't want to interfere with his morning. If his text had come in after one in the morning, there was no telling when he'd finally managed to get to sleep.

Several minutes later, a woman came to the door from inside and unlocked it. Not wanting to jump the gun, Rachel remained in her car, making sure she was still comfortable with what she had planned. As she waited, she watched as a man of about forty or so walked into the offices. Rachel watched through the window as the woman at the front desk greeted him with a smile.

After another few minutes, Rachel got out of the car and finally went inside. The same woman at the counter smiled at her but it wasn't genuine. Rachel figured she was probably good and tired of seeing her.

"Agent Gift, right?" the woman asked.

"Yes, that's right."

"Something else we can do for you?"

"Maybe so. So, we now strongly believe that the killer we're after somehow has access to your waiting list. And while we have the names and addresses, thanks to your cooperation, I was rather hoping that I could talk to a few of them. But instead of going down the list one by one—which would take a considerable amount of time—I was hoping you may be able to point me to a few that seem a little more hopeful than the others."

The question seemed to baffle the woman at first, but Rachel barely noticed. Instead, she was hung up on her own revelation. She was starting to understand that she personally needed to speak with those people—not for the case, but because of her own needs and internal struggles. She was one of them, whether she wanted to admit it or not. And now, on the cusp of agreeing to an experimental treatment with Dr. Emerson, she needed the encouragement.

"Well, I can only base what I know about our clients on my brief experiences with them as they check in and when I speak to them on the phone. If you need something deeper, you'd need to speak with some of our doctors or therapists."

This was an obstacle she'd been expecting, and the last thing Rachel wanted to do was take another deep dive into the tumultuous, rotten core that seemed to be at the center of Life Fulfilled.

"Surely there are records somewhere, right?" Rachel asked. "Anything with general remarks about the client's emotional stability or overall attitude?"

"There may be," the woman said, "but I'd need to make a call or two if that's the sort of thing you're looking for."

It wasn't the answer Rachel was hoping for, but it was better than nothing. As long as she didn't have to actually meet with any doctors or therapists, she'd be fine. If she absolutely had to, she supposed she could reach back out to Wes Dalton.

"That would be great for now," Rachel asked.

"And you know, there's a client here right now," the receptionist said. "He just came in a few minutes before you did. His name is Nick Nelson and he's sitting in the first room on the right. He's a little early for his nine thirty appointment. But he does that sometimes…comes in early to see if he can help out around here."

"Help?"

"Yes. He will sometimes help me file paperwork away—all things that don't have patient information on them, of course. He's swept, cleaned the windows, things like that." She chuckled and said, "So, now that I think about it, he may be the best person for you to speak with."

"Thank you," Rachel said.

She left the desk and headed down the short hallway. The door to the first room on the right was partially opened, but she knocked anyway.

"Yes?" a man's voice said from inside.

Rachel stepped in and found herself in a room that looked like the perfect mix of an office and a laidback lounge. All of the furniture was plump and colorful. The lighting was very low and almost sensual in a strange way. It was beyond relaxing, the sort of atmosphere that instantly put Rachel at ease.

And this was a good thing. The plan she had in place was to lie about her identity and maybe be a bit too honest about her current condition. So she'd be lying to a sick and potentially dying person while opening up a wound in herself that she was not yet comfortable with.

"Are you Nick Nelson?" she asked.

"I am," he said with a smile. "And you are?"

Nick Nelson was a good-looking man, maybe a bit older than forty. He was dressed in a collared shirt and a pair of nice, dark jeans. His dark hair was well-combed and held in place with a bit of product.

"My name is Abby Granger. I was thinking of trying to get on the waiting list. But I had some questions. I was hoping to talk to some clients before I pulled that trigger, you know?"

The first lie had been simple. Of course, if Nick Nelson and the receptionist ever spoke, her ruse would be broken. But by the time that ever happened, she'd be out of the building so she really didn't let it bother her.

"Oh, you poor thing," Nick said. "Do you mind if I ask what's wrong?"

"A tumor," she said with a sigh. "And it's in an area that makes it pretty much fatal to even try to remove it."

She felt stunned for a moment. It seemed to be getting easier to tell people, but telling the news to a complete stranger felt odd. It made her feel strangely vulnerable.

"Oh my God. I'm so sorry."

"It is what it is. I'm looking into an experimental treatment that I won't be able to afford, hence my visit here. Can I ask why you're here?"

"Colon cancer. From the way it's been explained to me, I have a few good weeks left before I'll start really falling apart. I've done some chemo had it's helped but…damn, do I hate chemo."

"I'm so sorry to hear that," Rachel said. "The lady up front said you sometimes come in early to help out around the place. Paperwork, janitorial stuff, things like that."

"Yeah, I do. I mean, they're a non-profit and they're doing so much for me. Helped me with some bills a few months back, providing rides to the hospital when I can't drive, that sort of thing. So I figure I should help them in any small way I can."

"Do you mind if I ask how long you've been with them?"

"Well, I cleared the waiting list a little over three months ago. I was on the waiting list for about six weeks. From what I hear, it's getting pretty long, so I guess I was lucky."

"Have you enjoyed working with the doctors and therapists?"

He considered this question for a moment and eventually nodded. "Yeah, I guess. It's weird because I feel bad for them…they're working so hard to make things comfortable for people they *know* are very likely going to die. It makes me…I don't know. It's why I do my best to help. Not only the people and offices of Life Fulfilled, but the other clients and the ones that are waiting. I mean, I know what that stress of hanging out on the waiting list is like. So whatever I can do to help, even in an unofficial capacity, I'm happy to do it."

"Well, it seems like you're keeping your spirits up," Rachel said. "Do you have family and friends in your corner to help?"

"No, not really. It's the main reason I decided to come to Life Fulfilled."

Another question formed on Rachel's tongue, but she kept it there. Something Nick said had struck her as odd, but she was only putting it together now. She tried to replay everything he'd said, trying to find what didn't seem right.

He seemed to sense her unease. He grew slightly rigid in his chair and even in the soft, ambient light and ease of the room, she felt the tension between them. He knew he'd said something he shouldn't have and simply stared at her, waiting.

"Well," she said, suddenly feeling the need to leave the room as quickly as possible, "I've bothered you enough. Thanks so much for answering my questions."

"Oh, it was no bother. I hope it all works out for you." He winked at her and said: "I'll put in a good word for you."

She smiled the best she could and then left the room. She replayed the last part of their conversation as she hurried by the front desk. She knew what it was now and it settled on her like a soiled blanket as she got back into her car.

It's why I do my best to help. Not only the people and offices of Life Fulfilled, but the other clients, and the ones that are waiting. I mean, I know what that stress of hanging out on the waiting list is like…

He was only a client. How would he have access to the waiting list?

Because he helps with filing, she told herself. *And even though the receptionist said it's all non-classified material, who's to say he didn't happen upon the waiting list somehow?*

Then, of course, there was the tension that had bloomed between them in the silence. He knew he'd slipped up and was waiting to see if she'd notice. When he saw that she *had* sensed something off, things had changed between them.

Now the one advantage she had going for her was that Nick Nelson thought that she was poor Abby Granger with a tumor in her head. He had no idea she was an FBI agent.

It's him, she thought. And before she could even bother to talk herself out of the notion, she grabbed her phone and called Jack. She knew she couldn't arrest him then and there, as she'd blatantly lied about her identity. But she could follow him and have Jack confront him and arrest him for mere suspicion.

It rang twice before he answered. "This is Agent Rivers."

"Jack, where are you?"

"On the way to the office. Why? Where are you? Did you get my t—"

"I've got our guy, Jack. I'm parked right outside Life Fulfilled and he's inside."

"How do you know?"

"Because I went inside to ask about a few clients under the pretense of being a possible client, looking for information. He was—"

She stopped here when she saw Nick Nelson come out of the Life Fulfilled building. He was moving quickly and looking directly across the street to where a parking garage took up the first quarter of the block. His speedy stride and the fact that he was exiting the building before his appointment suggested that his little slip-up, even to someone he had no reason to suspect was up to anything malicious, had rattled him a bit. And as far as Rachel was concerned, that was also an indicator of guilt.

"He's on the move, Jack. You're just going to have to trust me on this. I'm on leave, remember. No gun, no badge. He's…yeah, he's headed to the parking garage across the street."

"Rachel…if you really think this is him, *do not* engage. I'm on the way. Just try to keep an eye on him."

"Yeah, I'm already ahead of you."

"Okay. I'm on my way. And Rachel…please be smart about this."

"Always."

She ended the call and opened the driver's side door. When she looked across the street again, Nick Nelson had disappeared behind a column, heading for the stairs on the left side of the garage.

Rachel waited for a break in traffic before she crossed the street and then, just thirty seconds after Nelson had crossed in front of her car, she also entered the parking garage.

CHAPTER TWENTY NINE

The parking deck was comprised of three levels, the third serving as the uncovered roof. Because Rachel had spotted Nick Nelson heading to the left upon walking inside, she also went in that direction. The door to the stairway was there, closed and with no window or other break in it to see past it. Rachel recalled the speed with which Nick had come out of the Life Fulfilled building and couldn't imagine why he'd slow down coming through the parking garage. She highly doubted he knew she was on to him, that she was not Abby Granger but instead an FBI agent who had been hunting him down for the last two days. Given that, she doubted he was waiting behind that door, primed to attack her.

Opening it and quickly pivoting inside with her arms drawn up in a defensive fighting posture, she found that she was right. The stairwell was empty. She could, however, hear the faint sound of footsteps overhead and the sound of a heavy door either being pushed open or sliding closed on its hinges.

She hurried up the stairs, moving carefully so that her own footfalls would not be heard upstairs. When she came to the door, it was less than an inch from closing back into its frame. Rachel held her hand out to stop it and in a deft move, pushed it slightly open and slid out into the space of the second floor. Her right hand flinched as it fought the instinct to go for her Glock—a Glock that was, of course, not there.

The second level was just over half full. She figured there were thirty cars occupying roughly fifty spaces before a left-hand turn led to a ramp that stopped at the third level. What truly alarmed her, though, was that she did not see Nick Nelson. He couldn't have been any more than half a minute ahead of her when she'd entered the stairwell, but he seemed to have disappeared. Rachel stood still for a moment, listening for the sound of an engine starting. Maybe, she thought, he'd already gotten into his car.

But ten seconds passed and she heard no such thing. She walked out into the second level, walking directly in the center of the lane that separated the parking spots to her right and those to the left. She peered through the windows of every car she passed, looking for any sign of Nick Nelson simply sitting there, biding his time. But by the time she was halfway down the row, she'd not seen him and she also had not heard any engine starting up.

She took another step forward and froze in place as she heard a voice behind her. It was her name, in a whisper: *"Rachel."*

It came from behind her, somewhere every close by. This was unnerving because as she'd looked through the windows of the cars she'd passed by, she'd also looked to the spaces between the cars. She assumed Nelson could have easily been hiding by kneeling down in front of a car and then maneuvering around behind her. But as she turned around, she still didn't see him.

And just like that, she was no longer the one in pursuit; she was the one being pursued.

She thought of the "unofficial capacity" he'd spoken about and how he was trying to help those on a waiting list he should not have access to. It was more than enough to solidify in her mind the idea that he was indeed the killer. In his twisted mind, he was doing those people a service.

Then again, he'd just said her name—her *real* name. He knew somehow. But the question remained, did he believe everything she said to be a lie? Did he somehow have a radar within him that had latched on to her story about the tumor and knew it to be true, unlike the alias she'd given?

She turned, facing in the direction she'd heard his voice. There were two cars behind her and then a concrete pylon, a column that ran from the pavement to the girders along the underside of the third level. She eyed the cars carefully as she took two more steps forward and then her eyes went to the pylon. She clenched her fists, not sure what to prepare herself for.

And then she felt a dizzy spell coming on, pushed forward by a slight pulsing ache in her head.

No. No, not now…

She took a deep breath and summoned all of her focus and concentration. She knew that everything was riding on what might happen in the next few moments—catching a killer, closing this case. She'd told Jack she could get a handle on this, so now was the time to prove it. She focused on her breath, trying to lessen the way her adrenaline wanted to take control. She focused on the opening and closing of her fists, felt the breaths coming in and then pushing out of her body.

Slowly, the dizziness faded. The dull, pulsing ache remained, but it was virtually nothing, just a buzzing in the back of her head.

Not wanting to waste any more time, Rachel took a swift step to the side of the pylon, but there was nothing there to see. With her fists still clenched, she took a step back and when she did, she caught a blur of motion out of the corner of her left eye. She moved just in time to avoid the blow that was coming her way. As she dodged hard to the left, she saw Nick Nelson following through with his attack. There was something in his hand, a short, blunt object that looked like an old-fashioned club or lead sap. It struck the pylon with a loud *whack*. And then, realizing right away that he'd missed, he brought the club around in a back-handed attack.

She was so caught off guard and in the middle of her first dodge that Rachel was not able to completely dodge this blow. It struck her hard on the meat of her shoulder and sent her stumbling a bit.

Nelson came charging at her with the club raised over his shoulder. "I just want to help," he hissed while barreling ahead.

Still in mid-stumble, Rachel planted her hands on the pavement and kicked out hard with her right foot. It connected squarely with Nelson's hip, driving him back. He struck the bumper of a minivan and rebounded with a gasp as the breath went out of him. Still, he had the strength and wherewithal to lash out with another attack. But because he'd had the wind knocked out of him, there was very little strength behind it.

That was her single saving grace, as she was getting to her feet and regaining her balance. The club landed a glancing blow on the side of her head. It honestly didn't hurt all that much but the entire world instantly grew dizzy. She stumbled backwards again, her arms pinwheeling for balance.

Nelson surged forward, this time raising the club overhead. Rachel was seeing two of him and did her best to narrow her vision, squinting her eyes to find the open target of his throat. She delivered a hard right-handed jab that caught him just below the neck. Nelson dropped like a sack of bricks, gasping and coughing. Meanwhile, Rachel waved her hand out to find the pylon that she'd peered around just twenty or so seconds ago.

Just a few feet away, Nick Nelson was scrambling to his knees. Though Rachel did not have her full balance back, the world still reeling and rocking from the soft blow to her head, she advanced on him. She did her best to deliver a knee to his ribs and though she did make contact, she was also unable to stay on her feet.

Nelson screamed in agony as something in his side popped. Both of them fell to the pavement in a heap, Nelson's sap clattering around somewhere near Rachel's head. She reached for it and grabbed it, bringing it to her. She slowly made it to her knees again only to see that Nelson, still gasping and now heavily favoring his left side, was ambling away. He wasn't able to sprint, but had taken on a lopsided jog toward the stairwell door.

Rachel grunted and got to her feet. Her head was starting to pound a bit now and as she tried to follow after him, she wondered what sort of effects a blow to the head might have on someone with an inoperable tumor in their brain. The parking garage still seemed to be swaying all around her, but she did her best to stay within the lane between the two sides of the parking area.

Ahead, she saw Nelson open the door and enter the stairwell. She knew she had to get there quickly, not sure if he'd go up to the third floor or try an easier retreat down to the first. Yet as she closed in on the stairwell, she saw that she wasn't going to have to decide after all. She watched the door come flying open again as two men came bursting through it.

One was Nelson. The other was Jack. They were in a sort of Greco-Roman wrestling tangle. Slamming against the side wall of the garage, Nelson screamed again, but was also able to throw a punch that connected with Jack's face. Rachel rushed forward, and this time it was *she* who raised the club over her head.

Rather than connecting with his head and potentially killing him, she went low. Just as Nelson tried to start running away from Jack, she threw the club in a side-armed arc. It caught him directly between the shoulders and Nelson went sprawling to the pavement. Jack wasted no time, diving onto Nelson's back and starting the process of cuffing him.

"You're a liar!" Nelson screamed from underneath Jack. "You told me you were a patient…wanting to get on the waiting list! But you're with the FBI! At the front desk…I asked and she told me who you were and why you were there. You…but you're sick! I could see it. You were…you're *a liar*!"

Rachel ignored this as she leaned against the wall. Her vision slowly started to level out and she started to feel a central sort of throbbing where the club had struck her head.

"That's some great timing on your part," Rachel said.

"I know, right?" Jack said as he clicked the handcuffs closed around Nelson's wrists. "Now, how the hell did you know this was the guy?"

"I'll tell you on the way to HQ."

"You got a good story for Anderson, I hope."

“Shit. Forgot about that.”

“We’ll figure it out. You okay?”

“Yeah,” she said. The adrenaline was still rushing through her and she realized that it wasn’t even ten o’clock yet. So long as they could keep Anderson from finding out the part she’d played in this, she would be home very early, keeping her promise to Grandma Tate and Paige. “Yeah, I think I am.”

CHAPTER THIRTY

Rachel was back at home before noon. Jack had only let her get back behind the wheel of her car after making sure the fight with Nelson in the parking garage had really been as superficial as she was letting on. She'd found the house empty, with a note from Grandma Tate on the dry erase board hanging on the pantry door in the kitchen. It read: *Gym, then some grocery shopping, then back home. Should be back before Paige gets home from school.*

Rachel smiled. This meant that Grandma Tate had taken her at her word and assumed she would indeed be back home early in the day. She also liked the idea of Grandma Tate going to the gym, even if it was something like water aerobics or one of those pickleball leagues.

On the other hand, it was surreal to be sitting in her house less than an hour removed from a hand-to-hand fight with a killer in a parking garage. She spent a bit of time in the bathroom, making sure the slight whack to the side of the head had not caused bruising or swelling. She thought there might be the faintest bit of swelling, but it wasn't going to be noticed by anyone unless they were *really* staring at that side of her head.

Once she had calmed down a bit, getting a handle on the residual adrenaline and nerves, she sat down at the kitchen table with a cup of tea and a sandwich. She also had the thin folder with Dr. Emerson's information in it, including the little pamphlets that laid out the experimental procedures they'd talked about. She had no idea why she was so anxious to make the call. It was much easier than she'd anticipated, consisting of a very brief conversation with the first woman who answered the phone. After less than three minutes, she had an appointment set up with Dr. Emerson for the following week.

She tidied up a bit here and there just to occupy herself, but there wasn't much to do because Grandma Tate kept the house spotless when she had idle time. As she made her way through the house, Rachel ended up standing in the doorway of Paige's room. She looked inside and imagined that dead squirrel on the floor, placed there by order of Alex Lynch by a crony named Ed Walton.

She wondered, as she stared into her daughter's room, if she'd have such a difficult problem letting go of work if Alex Lynch wasn't free out there somewhere. If he hadn't escaped, would she be able to step away from her career a bit easier? She thought the answer was yes, but knowing that he was out there was unnerving. Deep down, she wondered how much longer the US Marshals and the FBI's resources would continue to look for him. She knew all too well how longstanding cases could often drift away and go stagnant if there wasn't some sort of movement within them from time to time.

She wasn't sure how long she'd been standing in Paige's doorway when there was a knock on the front door. She figured it couldn't be Grandma Tate because she had a key, so, curious, she made her way down as quickly as she could. She opened the front door just a crack at first and saw Jack standing there. She was relieved and, for a moment, wasn't sure why. Perhaps thoughts of Alex Lynch had made her think it would be him standing at her door.

Rachel opened the door for him and noticed right away that she looked nervous as he came inside. Jack normally wore an expression that was just a muscle twitch or two away from a smile. Now, though, he looked bothered by something—almost depressed.

"Everything okay?" she asked. "I thought you'd be deep into an interrogation with Nick Nelson by now."

"Yeah, that's coming up. But given that I was awake until damn near three a.m. last night and then brought Nelson in today, Anderson seemed perfectly happy to give me a chance to rest. He's got Lopez and Haskins talking to Nelson right now, sort of softening him up."

"And you chose to come here?" she asked.

"Yeah," he said. "I wanted to talk to you about something. Do you…do you mind if we sit down?"

"Sure, sure," she said, hurrying over to the couch. "Sorry. I'm not the best hostess."

"First of all, business first," Jack said as he sat down. "Nelson has already admitted to killing three people from the Life Fulfilled waiting list. He didn't seem proud of it, exactly, but there's no remorse there, either. He legitimately thinks he was doing them a favor. So you can rest easy in knowing that this one will be closed easily."

"And what about Anderson? Did he buy the story?"

"He did, and Lopez backed me up. Me calling for that backup was a genius move on your part. The story goes that I visited the Life Fulfilled offices, hoping to meet with some of the clients who had been selected off of the waiting list. And then it's basically *your* story, just with me in it and not you. Now, if it ever gets to the level where Nelson starts blabbing about how you fooled him, there could be questions.

Hell, he may even have a chance to walk. But with him actually admitting it, I doubt it. The case is pretty airtight."

"Sorry. I made this one a lot more complicated than it needed to be."

"Maybe. But you also caught our killer, so…" He shrugged, let out a sigh, and then looked her in the eyes. Again, she saw his nervousness and started to grow uncomfortable. "But that's not the entire reason I came. There's something else I need to tell you."

"Okay…"

"When you had it in your head that you weren't going to fight this, I wanted to help. I wanted to do anything I could. But it's a weird situation, you know? What can you do for someone who's been told they have about a year to live? And I could only think of one thing, and it's a little personal. Something you might actually get really mad at me about."

She had no idea what it could be and was starting to feel a bit scared and uncomfortable. "What is it, Jack? And please know, it would take a lot for me to get mad at you."

"Keep that in mind for the next twenty seconds or so, okay?"

She nodded and when she reached out to take his hand, hoping to calm him down, it felt a bit too natural. "You're starting to freak me out, Jack."

"I got in touch with your father," he said, blurting it out. "I know it wasn't my place, but there was just a moment a few weeks ago where I thought I had to. I had to do *something*. I remember you'd mentioned a few times that you had this estranged relationship with him and it was something you'd like to eventually patch up. So I did some digging, found his number, and called him."

For about half a second, she felt a wave of anger. It did feel like an intrusion of her privacy but as he continued to speak, she could see the sincerity in his eyes. He was so afraid that she was going to be mad at him that she couldn't help but feel a little honored that he'd taken such a step.

She squeezed his hand and released it. "It's okay," she said. "That's sort of sweet in a weird way, I guess. Did you actually talk to him?"

"I did. And he says he wants to meet you. Now, I didn't tell him everything that's going on because that's *really* not my place. But…well, if you want to talk to him, he's ready."

It was a scary feeling but she was also glad Jack had done this. It was sort of like ripping off a Band-Aid. The hard part was over and now she could play the rest out to her own wishes.

"How long ago was this?"

"A few days or so—before this case. I should have told you sooner, but I just didn't know when the right time would be. I had to do it today because it's been weighing on my mind heavily for the last few days. I was really afraid you be pissed. I just—"

"Jack."

He stopped and looked into her eyes, nodding. "Yeah, sorry."

"There's nothing to be sorry about."

She wasn't sure what else to say but she felt she had to say *something* because the longer they sat in silence, looking into one another's eyes, the more she wanted to kiss him. It was an urge that seemed to come out of nowhere and before she was aware of what she was doing, she leaned forward. Better sense took over in the last moment and she ended up barely getting his lips, kissing him instead on the very corner of his mouth.

He smiled at her as he pulled away and she did her best not to grin when she noticed him blushing. "It was a sweet gesture," she said. "And if you still have his number, I might just reach out to him."

"I do. So just ask when you think you're ready. He knows the ball is very much in your court now."

Another silence fell between them and this time it was Jack who seemed to notice it first. He got to his feet. "I better get back to the interrogation room," he said. "I'm afraid the longer I'm gone, the more likely Nelson will be to confuse other agents about the real story of what happened."

"Yeah, good idea. Oh…and Jack?"

He looked back at her and she caught bit of hopeful mischief in his eyes. She could tell he wanted her to kiss him again—and this time more than just a side-of-the-mouth peck. "Yeah?"

"I called Emerson today. I've got an appointment to meet with him about starting his experimental treatment next Wednesday."

His smile was instant. It lit up his face. Hell, it lit up the entire room. "That's great news, Rachel."

"Yeah, I'm hoping so. Look…maybe give me a call in a day or two. Let me know how this all plays out."

"Sure thing," he said as he made his way to the door. And when he opened it, they stared at one another for a handful of seconds, moments that made Rachel wonder just how long this little spark had laid dormant between them.

When he closed the door behind him, Rachel settled back down on the couch. And for the first time in a very long time, she smiled as she thought about her father.

***

Over the next two days, she received updates about the Nick Nelson case via texts from Jack. They learned how he'd managed to get a copy of the waiting list by saving it to a USB one day while he'd been at Life Fulfilled under the guise of cleaning the windows. He also got very detailed about how he'd staked each victim out and that he was prepared to do so until either he died or he ran out of people on the list.

His claim of having colon cancer was true. They had his medical records on file and Nelson's doctor's statement that Nelson might have about two years to live if he continued with his treatment but the cancer would eventually kill him. Because of that, there was much debate about what sort of facility Nelson should spend his final days in.

It was on the evening of the second day that Jack actually called her. Paige was getting ready for bed, Grandma Tate was out at the local library testing out a book club, and Rachel was sitting on the back porch with a glass of white wine. She was worried that things might be odd between them after the tense moment in her living room two days ago, but as they started talking it seemed they didn't miss a beat.

After basic catching-up, Jack veered into Nick Nelson's case. "It's just as well that you aren't here for this," he said. "The debate about if he goes to a standard prison but a safer ward or to a medical and psychiatric facility is a heated one. It's getting a little out of hand. But because of this debate and his admission of killing three people, the finer details of how he was caught are pretty minor."

"That's good. And thanks for managing all of that."

"Of course."

"Now, what about Alex Lynch? Have you heard anything at all about the progress of the hunt for him?"

"Funny you should ask. I was talking to one of the guys who are organizing that hunt, working with the US Marshals today. I painted it as simple curiosity, given that you're my partner and Lynch is sort of connected to you. He said the last update they got was yesterday afternoon, right around lunchtime. They suspect he's in Georgia. They're following some leads and he's still on the run."

"Georgia. That's good. That's a good distance away. But they don't know where he's headed?"

"Not that I know of. And the way this guy talked, Georgia is just speculation. The Savannah branch got a few calls about a man they believed to be Lynch but nothing has been confirmed yet. You should also know, though, that Anderson is still having the occasional car swing by your place just to keep an eye on things."

"That's sweet of him, but unnecessary."

"I don't know that I've ever heard anyone refer to Anderson as *sweet*."

"Thanks for the updates, Jack. Don't be a stranger. Feel free to swing by anytime you like."

"I might just take you up on that. How about you? Your two-week leave is rapidly only becoming one. You think you'll be coming back?"

She looked out to the back yard where Paige had left her hula hoop and soccer ball. Rachel had gone out and attempted to hula hoop for the first time in about twenty years. She'd broken a sweat and nearly cried from laughing.

"I don't know yet," she said.

They ended the call and Rachel headed back inside. It was a special night, as she took the time to read to Paige and they snuggled in bed together without worry or tears. With the exception of Peter not being in the house, it almost felt like normal. She kissed Paige goodnight and headed downstairs only to find that Grandma Tate had come back from her book club while Rachel had been upstairs.

"Did you like it?" Rachel asked.

"Oh, sure. It was fine, I suppose. Never been much of a reader."

"Then why a book club?"

"Because I want to try something different. Even by beating this cancer I'm *still* old. Might as well get stuff done while I can, right?"

Rachel's cell phone started to ring as she laughed at this. "That's a little morbid, Grandma."

She didn't bother checking the caller ID, as she was distracted by Grandma Tate. She also assumed it would be Jack again, maybe with another update on Nick Nelson.

"Hello?" she asked.

"Hello," came the reply. And for a moment, she thought it *was* Jack. But no, it was deeper and older, maybe a little grizzled. Her dad, maybe? She'd still not decided how to approach that situation ever since Jack had laid that pleasant little bomb at her feet. "This is Agent Gift, yes?"

"It is," she asked. "Who is this?"

The man on the other end chuckled. It was a deadly, dry sound. "Oh, I think you know who it is. And I'm coming for you. I'm coming for you soon."

Lynch.

She gripped her phone tightly as fear and anger created a massive wall of determination inside of her. "You're very stupid to be calling here, Ly—"

"So what book is your grandmother's book club reading? Something good, I hope."

"How do you—"

"The woman in the blue windbreaker that was sitting beside her didn't seem too pleased with the book selection."

"What are—"

"See you soon, Rachel."

The line went dead and Rachel looked around the living room, her eyes instantly going to the lock on the front door. She then looked to the book Grandma Tate had set on the coffee table, the book she'd be reading for her book club.

How does he know? It was a loaded question and one that Rachel was a bit too scared to answer.

"Who was that?" Grandma Tate asked.

"Grandma, who was sitting beside you at the book club?"

She answered, though it was clear that she was confused by the question. "A woman I had never met before. A lady named Katherine…oh, I don't recall her last name. Why?"

"What was she wearing?"

"I don't recall," she said, growing concerned.

"Did she have on a windbreaker?" Rachel asked. "A blue windbreaker?"

"Now that you mention it…yes. She even made a comment about how she was glad she decided to wear it because it was a bit chilly in the room." She paused here and then asked again: "Rachel…who was that on the phone?"

"That," Rachel said, "was Alex Lynch. And he's a lot closer to us than we thought."

HER LAST BREATH
(A Rachel Gift FBI Suspense Thriller —Book 6)

When a serial killer strikes a seemingly random group of middle-aged men, Rachel's skills are truly put to the test. She must enter the killer's twisted mind and find the thread connecting them all—before time runs out.

FBI Special Agent Rachel Gift is among the FBI's most brilliant agents at hunting down serial killers. She plans on doing this forever—until she discovers she has months left to live. Determined to go down fighting, and to keep her diagnosis a secret, Rachel faces her own mortality while trying to save other's lives. But how long can she go until she collapses under the weight of it all?

"A MASTERPIECE OF THRILLER AND MYSTERY. Blake Pierce did a magnificent job developing characters with a psychological side so well described that we feel inside their minds, follow their fears and cheer for their success. Full of twists, this book will keep you awake until the turn of the last page."
--Books and Movie Reviews, Roberto Mattos (re Once Gone)

HER LAST BREATH (A Rachel Gift FBI Suspense Thriller) is book #6 in a long-anticipated new series by #1 bestseller and USA Today bestselling author Blake Pierce, whose bestseller Once Gone (a free download) has received over 1,000 five star reviews.

FBI Agent Rachel Gift, 33, unparalleled for her ability to enter the minds of serial killers, is a rising star in the Behavioral Crimes Unit—until a routine doctor visit reveals she has but a few months left to live.

Not wishing to burden others with her pain, Rachel decides, agonizing as it is, not to tell anyone—not even her boss, her partner, her husband, or her seven-year-old daughter. She wants to go down fighting, and to take as many serial killers with her as she can.

A string of seemingly-unconnected murders has Rachel baffled—but she can't afford to freeze. Facing a case more difficult than any she's seen before, Rachel must use her brilliant mind to piece together the clues before time runs out.

Can she find uncover the connection between the victims before the killer outsmarts her?

A riveting and chilling crime thriller featuring a brilliant and flailing FBI agent, the RACHEL GIFT series is an unputdownable mystery, packed with suspense, twists and shocking secrets, propelled by a page-turning pace that will keep you bleary-eyed late into the night.

Books #6-#8 are also available!

Blake Pierce

Blake Pierce is the USA Today bestselling author of the RILEY PAGE mystery series, which includes seventeen books. Blake Pierce is also the author of the MACKENZIE WHITE mystery series, comprising fourteen books; of the AVERY BLACK mystery series, comprising six books; of the KERI LOCKE mystery series, comprising five books; of the MAKING OF RILEY PAIGE mystery series, comprising six books; of the KATE WISE mystery series, comprising seven books; of the CHLOE FINE psychological suspense mystery, comprising six books; of the JESSE HUNT psychological suspense thriller series, comprising twenty four books; of the AU PAIR psychological suspense thriller series, comprising three books; of the ZOE PRIME mystery series, comprising six books; of the ADELE SHARP mystery series, comprising fifteen books, of the EUROPEAN VOYAGE cozy mystery series, comprising four books; of the new LAURA FROST FBI suspense thriller, comprising nine books (and counting); of the new ELLA DARK FBI suspense thriller, comprising eleven books (and counting); of the A YEAR IN EUROPE cozy mystery series, comprising nine books, of the AVA GOLD mystery series, comprising six books (and counting); of the RACHEL GIFT mystery series, comprising eight books (and counting); of the VALERIE LAW mystery series, comprising nine books (and counting); of the PAIGE KING mystery series, comprising six books (and counting); of the MAY MOORE mystery series, comprising six books (and counting); and the CORA SHIELDS mystery series, comprising three books (and counting).

An avid reader and lifelong fan of the mystery and thriller genres, Blake loves to hear from you, so please feel free to visit www.blakepierceauthor.com to learn more and stay in touch.

HER LAST FEAR (Book #4)
HER LAST CHOICE (Book #5)
HER LAST BREATH (Book #6)
HER LAST MISTAKE (Book #7)
HER LAST DESIRE (Book #8)

AVA GOLD MYSTERY SERIES
CITY OF PREY (Book #1)
CITY OF FEAR (Book #2)
CITY OF BONES (Book #3)
CITY OF GHOSTS (Book #4)
CITY OF DEATH (Book #5)
CITY OF VICE (Book #6)

A YEAR IN EUROPE
A MURDER IN PARIS (Book #1)
DEATH IN FLORENCE (Book #2)
VENGEANCE IN VIENNA (Book #3)
A FATALITY IN SPAIN (Book #4)

ELLA DARK FBI SUSPENSE THRILLER
GIRL, ALONE (Book #1)
GIRL, TAKEN (Book #2)
GIRL, HUNTED (Book #3)
GIRL, SILENCED (Book #4)
GIRL, VANISHED (Book 5)
GIRL ERASED (Book #6)
GIRL, FORSAKEN (Book #7)
GIRL, TRAPPED (Book #8)
GIRL, EXPENDABLE (Book #9)
GIRL, ESCAPED (Book #10)
GIRL, HIS (Book #11)

LAURA FROST FBI SUSPENSE THRILLER
ALREADY GONE (Book #1)
ALREADY SEEN (Book #2)
ALREADY TRAPPED (Book #3)
ALREADY MISSING (Book #4)
ALREADY DEAD (Book #5)
ALREADY TAKEN (Book #6)

ALREADY CHOSEN (Book #7)
ALREADY LOST (Book #8)
ALREADY HIS (Book #9)

EUROPEAN VOYAGE COZY MYSTERY SERIES
MURDER (AND BAKLAVA) (Book #1)
DEATH (AND APPLE STRUDEL) (Book #2)
CRIME (AND LAGER) (Book #3)
MISFORTUNE (AND GOUDA) (Book #4)
CALAMITY (AND A DANISH) (Book #5)
MAYHEM (AND HERRING) (Book #6)

ADELE SHARP MYSTERY SERIES
LEFT TO DIE (Book #1)
LEFT TO RUN (Book #2)
LEFT TO HIDE (Book #3)
LEFT TO KILL (Book #4)
LEFT TO MURDER (Book #5)
LEFT TO ENVY (Book #6)
LEFT TO LAPSE (Book #7)
LEFT TO VANISH (Book #8)
LEFT TO HUNT (Book #9)
LEFT TO FEAR (Book #10)
LEFT TO PREY (Book #11)
LEFT TO LURE (Book #12)
LEFT TO CRAVE (Book #13)
LEFT TO LOATHE (Book #14)
LEFT TO HARM (Book #15)

THE AU PAIR SERIES
ALMOST GONE (Book#1)
ALMOST LOST (Book #2)
ALMOST DEAD (Book #3)

ZOE PRIME MYSTERY SERIES
FACE OF DEATH (Book#1)
FACE OF MURDER (Book #2)
FACE OF FEAR (Book #3)
FACE OF MADNESS (Book #4)
FACE OF FURY (Book #5)

FACE OF DARKNESS (Book #6)

A JESSIE HUNT PSYCHOLOGICAL SUSPENSE SERIES
THE PERFECT WIFE (Book #1)
THE PERFECT BLOCK (Book #2)
THE PERFECT HOUSE (Book #3)
THE PERFECT SMILE (Book #4)
THE PERFECT LIE (Book #5)
THE PERFECT LOOK (Book #6)
THE PERFECT AFFAIR (Book #7)
THE PERFECT ALIBI (Book #8)
THE PERFECT NEIGHBOR (Book #9)
THE PERFECT DISGUISE (Book #10)
THE PERFECT SECRET (Book #11)
THE PERFECT FAÇADE (Book #12)
THE PERFECT IMPRESSION (Book #13)
THE PERFECT DECEIT (Book #14)
THE PERFECT MISTRESS (Book #15)
THE PERFECT IMAGE (Book #16)
THE PERFECT VEIL (Book #17)
THE PERFECT INDISCRETION (Book #18)
THE PERFECT RUMOR (Book #19)
THE PERFECT COUPLE (Book #20)
THE PERFECT MURDER (Book #21)
THE PERFECT HUSBAND (Book #22)
THE PERFECT SCANDAL (Book #23)
THE PERFECT MASK (Book #24)

CHLOE FINE PSYCHOLOGICAL SUSPENSE SERIES
NEXT DOOR (Book #1)
A NEIGHBOR'S LIE (Book #2)
CUL DE SAC (Book #3)
SILENT NEIGHBOR (Book #4)
HOMECOMING (Book #5)
TINTED WINDOWS (Book #6)

KATE WISE MYSTERY SERIES
IF SHE KNEW (Book #1)
IF SHE SAW (Book #2)

IF SHE RAN (Book #3)
IF SHE HID (Book #4)
IF SHE FLED (Book #5)
IF SHE FEARED (Book #6)
IF SHE HEARD (Book #7)

THE MAKING OF RILEY PAIGE SERIES
WATCHING (Book #1)
WAITING (Book #2)
LURING (Book #3)
TAKING (Book #4)
STALKING (Book #5)
KILLING (Book #6)

RILEY PAIGE MYSTERY SERIES
ONCE GONE (Book #1)
ONCE TAKEN (Book #2)
ONCE CRAVED (Book #3)
ONCE LURED (Book #4)
ONCE HUNTED (Book #5)
ONCE PINED (Book #6)
ONCE FORSAKEN (Book #7)
ONCE COLD (Book #8)
ONCE STALKED (Book #9)
ONCE LOST (Book #10)
ONCE BURIED (Book #11)
ONCE BOUND (Book #12)
ONCE TRAPPED (Book #13)
ONCE DORMANT (Book #14)
ONCE SHUNNED (Book #15)
ONCE MISSED (Book #16)
ONCE CHOSEN (Book #17)

MACKENZIE WHITE MYSTERY SERIES
BEFORE HE KILLS (Book #1)
BEFORE HE SEES (Book #2)
BEFORE HE COVETS (Book #3)
BEFORE HE TAKES (Book #4)
BEFORE HE NEEDS (Book #5)
BEFORE HE FEELS (Book #6)

BEFORE HE SINS (Book #7)
BEFORE HE HUNTS (Book #8)
BEFORE HE PREYS (Book #9)
BEFORE HE LONGS (Book #10)
BEFORE HE LAPSES (Book #11)
BEFORE HE ENVIES (Book #12)
BEFORE HE STALKS (Book #13)
BEFORE HE HARMS (Book #14)

AVERY BLACK MYSTERY SERIES
CAUSE TO KILL (Book #1)
CAUSE TO RUN (Book #2)
CAUSE TO HIDE (Book #3)
CAUSE TO FEAR (Book #4)
CAUSE TO SAVE (Book #5)
CAUSE TO DREAD (Book #6)

KERI LOCKE MYSTERY SERIES
A TRACE OF DEATH (Book #1)
A TRACE OF MURDER (Book #2)
A TRACE OF VICE (Book #3)
A TRACE OF CRIME (Book #4)
A TRACE OF HOPE (Book #5)